This simply wouldn't do!

Tansy lifted her head from his shoulder. 'That was rather a shock,' she excused herself unsteadily. 'So yet again, I have to thank you for being so kind.'

'Yes, it's astonishing how often I seem to give you cause to do that,' Struan returned thoughtfully. 'But what puzzles me is why you always sound so surprised.'

How could she tell him it was because she found him more considerate than the brother he resembled?

Dear Reader

This month we offer you Accident and Emergency, Cardiac, Physiotherapy, and a holiday resort in Egypt — how's that for variety? Lynne Collins gives us a hero who is dogged by gossip, Lilian Darcy an older heroine coping with passion for a younger man, Drusilla Douglas a heroine confused by identical twins, and Margaret Barker gives us a pair who had met before. . .

We hope you enjoy learning how they solve their problems!

The Editor

Drusilla Douglas is a physiotherapist who has written numerous short stories — mainly for Scottish-based magazines. Now the luxury of working part-time has provided her with the leisure necessary for writing novels.

Recent titles by the same author:

A BORDER PRACTICE
SURGEON'S STRATEGY

A DOUBLE DOSE

BY

DRUSILLA DOUGLAS

MILLS & BOON LIMITED
ETON HOUSE   18–24 PARADISE ROAD
RICHMOND   SURREY   TW9 1SR

*First published in Great Britain 1993
by Mills & Boon Limited*

© Drusilla Douglas 1993

*Australian copyright 1993
Philippine copyright 1993
This edition 1993*

ISBN 0 263 78344 8

*Set in 10 on 11½ pt Linotron Times
03-9309-55359*

*Typeset in Great Britain by Centracet, Cambridge
Made and printed in Great Britain*

CHAPTER ONE

'MISS NICHOLSON,' said the senior medical registrar in his deep, resonant voice, startling Tansy into spilling ice all over the treatment-room floor.

'You made me jump, Dr McLeod,' she accused.

'So it would seem — my apologies, then. I only wanted to ask whether or not you'd done Mrs Clarke's muscle test.'

'Um — no — not yet. Mr Cox did say as long as I had it for the round on Friday, so I thought — '

'Fine usually, but since then our revered consultant, Dr Tait, has arranged for her to be seen by his opposite number in Neurology. Tomorrow morning.'

That put a different complexion on things. 'In that case, I'll have my findings in the case-notes by five o'clock today, Doctor,' Tansy promised rashly.

'Good girl.' Those smoky blue eyes of his, which the student nurses thought were so sexy, were now surveying the watery mess spreading over the floor. 'I'd clean that up if I were you, lassie,' he advised. 'Sister's not in the best of moods today.'

When was she ever? 'I intended to,' protested Tansy, but he was already striding off down the corridor. 'I hate you, Struan McLeod,' she muttered with more fervour than truth. It was actually his identical twin brother Calum whom Tansy hated.

No time for brooding now, though, with Sister Aitken having replaced the senior registrar in the doorway. 'What are you doing on your hands and knees, girl?' she demanded.

'I spilled some ice and it made rather a mess, Sister.'

'Hmm! Better not to have spilled it at all, don't you think?'

'Oh, *much* better, Sister!' You—you nasty old female person, you!

'Well, don't do it again!' That said, Sister Aitken stomped off. To find somebody else to torment, no doubt.

She was virtually the last survivor of the old guard who believed that if you didn't constantly squash the young staff all hell would break loose within the hallowed walls of Edinburgh's famous Royal Alexandra Infirmary. Tansy was still smarting from the dressing-down she'd received on her very first day on Ward Eighteen. That was a week ago today, but it felt more like a year. And all for exchanging Christian names with a nervous girl patient, hardly older than herself. But never mind, Tansy, girl, only eleven weeks to go and you'll be free of old Mighty Mouse.

Sister Aitken was five feet nothing in her rubber-soled Barker's shoes, and rumour had it that it was Dr Tait himself who had given her her nickname while still a lowly houseman. And never forget this is all your own fault, Tansy. If you hadn't gone charging home to work in private practice the minute you qualified—and much good *that* did you!—you'd have finished the post-grad trail round every unit by now and be on the next rung of the ladder. But that was another story.

Tansy wrung out the floorcloth, got to her feet and emptied the bucket of dirty water into the sink.

'Have you done anything about Mrs Baird's icebath yet, Tansy?' asked Bill Cox, the senior physiotherapist on the medical unit, taking his turn to pause in the doorway.

'It's just about ready,' Tansy claimed optimistically. 'I had a sort of hiccup—spilled some ice. . .'

'Easily done,' he sympathised. 'Now listen. I've got to leave this ward for a bit, but you'll find me in Twenty if you need me. Yet another post-flu chest infection for ventilating, would you believe? I'll be glad when this winter's over.'

Me too, thought Tansy, as the sound of his footsteps died away. Come the daffodils, and I'll not have Struan McLeod conjuring up painful memories every time I set eyes on him. . . Oh, do stop mooning, you wimp, and get on with the work.

'My word, but that's cold, love,' gasped Mrs Baird as she sank her spastic hand in the swirling, icy mass.

'You'll forget that, though, when you see how your fingers uncurl,' promised Tansy soothingly. 'How long did you say it is since your stroke?'

'Two years—more or less. I was all right while I was going for the therapy, but after Jim's mother came to stay with us I couldn't seem to find the time. She gets lonely if she's left on her own too long—and she needs such a lot of attention.'

No wonder the poor wee soul had seized up. Getting pneumonia and having to be admitted to hospital had been a blessing in disguise. Now she was having what Dr Tait called some 'intensive revving up' and would be going home much more mobile than she'd been for months. 'Surely your mother-in-law can't complain of loneliness in that old folks' home she's in just now?' supposed Tansy.

'She hates it—and she's dying to get back to us. She told Jim that nobody takes any notice of her.'

More likely nobody dances attendance on her the way you did, guessed Tansy, wondering if she'd be exceeding her authority by advising Jim Baird to leave his mother where she was if he valued his wife's health. 'See — what did I tell you? Your fingers are nearly straight now,' she pointed out. 'A good passive stretch, and then we'll try some exercises.'

Both physio and patient were pleased with that session, after which Tansy moved on to treat her share of the chest cases which always figured so largely on the physio list in a medical ward. Three of them would require another treatment before Tansy went off duty, and there was still that manual muscle test to be done. And she hadn't done one of those since goodness knew when. Mustn't mess it up. . .

Gauging the approximate strength of each muscle on a scale of nought to five wasn't too difficult, but, with both legs to be tested and the patient — heavy as well as weak — protesting bitterly every time Tansy had to change her position, the test took nearly an hour to complete. So it was getting on for six before she finished work for the day.

Thankfully she said, 'Goodnight,' to her last patient and drew back the cubicle curtains to reveal Sister Aitken, wearing a glare that would have unsettled a battle-hardened marine. 'You are a very slow worker, Miss Nicholson,' she pronounced scornfully.

Suddenly Tansy decided that she'd had enough of this harassment. Of course one wanted to keep on the right side of the ward sister, but it was Bill Cox, not Mighty Mouse, who was Tansy's immediate superior. 'I've had fifteen treatments to give this afternoon, Sister,' she began politely but firmly, 'as well as a very time-consuming muscle test at Dr Tait's particular request.'

That last had been a piece of pure inspiration, when all doctors were gods in Sister Aitken's book. 'Oh — ah, hum!' she sniffed. 'But it's nearly time for the suppers to be given out, so don't let it happen again.'

How did she think anybody could promise that it wouldn't? She's bonkers, decided Tansy, going on to consolidate her ascendancy. 'As it's the doctors who decide which patients a physio should treat, I'm in no position to promise that,' she returned quietly, scuttling off before Sister recovered from the shock of being spoken back to.

From the treatment-room, Tansy collected the bulky canister in which ice was transported daily from the physiotherapy department to the ward. On the way back to base, she met her best friend, Kirsty Faulds, who promptly offered to take a handle.

'You've very late tonight, Tansy — and looking gey trachled as well,' Kirsty noted candidly.

'So would you after two brushes with old Mighty Mouse in the one afternoon,' sighed Tansy. 'Anyway, you're not exactly early yourself.'

'I know — our ward round went on longer than usual.' Kirsty was now senior assistant physio on General Surgery. 'And me due to meet my beloved in twenty minutes too,' she added with a sigh.

Kirsty's fiancé, Hamish Cullen, was a registrar in paediatrics at Edinburgh's other big hospital. They were getting married at Easter and were in a hectic flurry of house-hunting.

'So what are you inspecting tonight, then?' asked Tansy. 'That bargain flat in Stockbridge?'

'No, a modern desres up at Fairmilehead. It's freezing cold and over-snowed up there in winter, but, on the other hand, it'd be very handy for Hamish when he's on call.'

'I'll think of you enjoying yourself, then, while I'm

slaving away here,' said Tansy in a poor-little-me voice. She was on call that night.

'Poor old Tans!' exclaimed Kirsty as they turned into Physiotherapy and headed for the preparation-room to get rid of their burden. 'It's all work and no play for you just now. You know, it really is time to think about finding yourself another man.'

Tansy knew that just fine. The trouble was that the only man Tansy had ever wanted was Calum McLeod — and he had stopped wanting her suddenly and agonisingly last summer. Lately, she'd thought she was getting herself together again. Until she had started on Medical last week, encountering Calum's identical twin every damn day since. 'One day, Kirsty, one day,' she promised vaguely as they set down the canister. She rubbed her aching biceps. 'First things first, though. Now to find out what's on the cards for tonight.'

The list pinned to the noticeboard did nothing to cheer her. Four in Intensive Care, six on the cardiothoracic unit, six — no, seven — on Surgical. And that was without any emergencies. There was no point in going home first, so Tansy decided to sample supper in the staff canteen.

Having collected a tired-looking salad from the cold cabinet, she looked around for somewhere to sit. Only a few tables were used in the evenings and, as Sister Aitken had already commandeered one, Tansy sat down as far from her as she could get, hoping not to be noticed. A folded copy of the *Scotsman* and a half-eaten meal congealing on a plate suggested that somebody else had had the same idea, and Tansy hoped that her unknown colleague wouldn't object. The way her luck was running these days, she'd probably picked a chair next to a consultant!

But it was Struan McLeod who presently slid into the vacant seat. 'Oh, dear,' said Tansy.

He eyed her with surprise and a tinge of reproach before glancing at her plate. 'I get your point,' he assumed wrongly. 'Not exactly *haute cuisine*, is it?' He frowned down at his own plate before pushing it aside and remarking, 'That phone call must have taken longer than I thought. So what's that like?' he asked unhopefully.

'What's what like, Doctor?' asked Tansy.

'Your salad. It looks as though it had died of exhaustion.'

Despite her resentment of him for being Calum's brother, for looking exactly like him and just for being there, Tansy had to smile.

'It's not the nicest meal I've ever had,' she agreed, 'but, on balance, the best that's going.' While trying to spear a piece of squashy tomato, she happened to encounter Sister Aitken's outraged glare. 'Oh, dear,' she said again. 'Sister is giving me dreadful looks and I'm sure it's because I'm sitting at your table. I think I'd better move.'

'That's a pity,' he said, 'but if it'll make you any happier, I'll go and sit somewhere else once I've traded in this mess for a sandwich.' And with that, he got to his feet, picked up his plate and his newspaper, and strode off towards the servery.

Tansy watched him go. He even walks like Calum, she realised with a little pang. Neither brother was exceptionally tall—five ten at most—but that was a good height for twins and each had a very good pair of shoulders on him.

Vividly, Tansy recalled the first time she had ever seen Calum. It was during her last year at college and she had gone home to the farm in Fife for a weekend

of serious swotting. Going out to the byre to call her
father in for his lunch on the Sunday, she had found,
not him, but their veterinary surgeon's new assistant,
Calum McLeod. He had stripped to the waist to deliver
a calf and the sight of his rippling shoulder muscles had
been all it had taken to make Tansy fall headlong in
love for the very first time. The young vet had liked the
look of her too and Tansy had just known she had
found her Mr Right. Yet, six months later, he had
dumped her. She closed her eyes against such painful
recollections.

When she opened them again, she saw that Calum's
brother was now sitting at the next table, his sandwich
neglected while he chatted up the pretty radiographer
seated opposite. Tansy frowned. There was absolutely
no difference between the twins. Same curly dark hair,
healthy tanned skin, dancing blue eyes, straight nose,
clefted chin. . . Never trust a man with a dimple in his
chin, Granny Nicholson had been fond of saying, and,
on experience to date, she was dead right.

Against her better judgement, Tansy stole another
look. Perhaps Struan's face was marginally thinner, the
line of cheek and jaw more firmly drawn, more definite
than his brother's. Or was she merely clutching at
straws, seeing differences where none existed, just
because she couldn't think how she was to endure
seeing the face of the man she had worshipped every
day for the next eleven weeks?

But maudlin masochism wasn't really Tansy's style
and her common sense soon revived. Here was one
instance of seeing when she needn't. She'd be far better
to eat up, get out of the canteen, and start the evening
stint.

Newly qualified physiotherapists were always closely
supervised by their seniors. With her time in private

practice behind her, Tansy had passed the reliability test quite early, but this was the first time she'd been allowed to work unsupervised on evening duty. That alone was enough to keep her mind off her troubles for the next few hours.

Ten o'clock found her drooping wearily at the nursing station on the intensive care unit, waiting to be told whether she'd be needed there again that night.

The duty doctor raised her hopes with a negative, only to depress them next minute when he said, 'But we put a nice old chap in Ward Twenty on to a ventilator this morning, and he could probably do with some of your help. I'm going across to see him now. Do you mind coming too?'

Naturally Tansy told him 'Of course not,' and they set off for Medical, which was on the other side of the car park. At this hour, it was almost empty as well as rather eerie on this cold, misty February night. Ward Twenty was on the top floor and the lift was out of order, causing the anaesthetist to swear wearily as they plodded up the stairs.

As he had predicted, Mr McKenna's chest was very moist and he definitely needed physio to clear it, but, as he said after examining the patient, it would have been worse had Tansy got home only to be called out again.

Treating a patient on a ventilator was fairly straight-forward, though the patient on the receiving end would probably put it more forcefully. It was necessary to turn him gently, first on one side and then the other, squeezing and shaking the ribcage to propel the secretions upwards towards the trachea, to remove them by means of suction. Mr McKenna's special nurse did that, while Tansy did the vibrations. It was little more than five minutes' work, and now, at last, Tansy could go home. From Physio, she rang for a taxi, because nocturnal transport for female staff without a car was on the NHS. This wasn't quite the extravagance it sounded, when lone women waiting for buses in the middle of the night were all too often misunderstood and attacked as fair game by warped sex-seekers too mean to pay a professional.

Her luck in for once, Tansy's taxi arrived at the instant she reached the porters' lodge, and ten minutes after that she was opening the door of the top flat on the other side of the park, which she shared with Kirsty.

An hour or two later, she was awakened by the shriek of the telephone, which could only mean one thing. Yawning and blinking, Tansy stumbled out to the hall. 'Duty physio? Look, I'm awfully sorry,' said the night staff nurse on Twenty. 'I know you've already been to Mr McKenna once tonight, but Doctor is asking for him to have another treatment.'

'It's all right — I'll be there as soon as I can get a taxi,' promised Tansy.

Some time later, having treated the patient, Tansy had to agree that the doctor in question had not been over-reacting. 'I just can't think where it's all coming from,' she said. 'I bet you wish you could make money as quickly, Mr McKenna.'

Of course he couldn't answer, not with that great tube sticking out of his mouth, but he winked his appreciation of her attempt to lighten the atmosphere. 'I think he'll need treating again before morning,' Tansy said in a low voice to the nurse as they washed their hands afterwards.

The girl agreed. 'But the doctor's still in the office if you want to check,' she revealed.

Tansy said what a good idea that was, but changed her mind when she saw that the doctor sitting at the desk was the senior registrar. The staff nurse who had called her in was tenderly plying him with tea and toast and Tansy fancied that they weren't too pleased at being interrupted. 'So sorry, Dr McLeod,' she apologised, 'but when Mr McKenna's nurse told me you were still here, I thought I may as well ask if he'll be needing another treatment before morning.'

'What do you think?' asked Struan McLeod.

Junior physiotherapists were rarely asked for an opinion, and Tansy was flummoxed. 'Well, I. . . He's certainly filling up fairly quickly, so I suppose the answer is yes. Probably about six. . .'

'You're absolutely right. Look, I'm sorry you're having such a bad time,' he insisted with a dazzling smile that was too much like Calum's to be appreicated. 'Tell you what, I'll leave a note for the houseman to check him before waking you—just in case it's not necessary. That's the best I can do for you, I'm afraid.'

'And very thoughtful too,' Tansy had to allow. 'But I don't think I'll bother going back to bed. It's hardly worth it.'

'You're still fairly new to this game, but you will if you've any sense,' he advised. 'Nobody's going to thank you for falling asleep on the job tomorrow.'

'Least of all Mighty Mouse,' returned Tansy unguardedly.

At that, Struan McLeod smiled again, displaying teeth just as white and even as his brother's. 'Just so,' he chuckled. 'Well, goodnight for now, then, Miss Nicholson.'

Back in Physio, Tansy took his advice and went to bed in the room kept for just this situation. She cursed him roundly though when the phone went just as she was putting out the light. This time it was Intensive Care calling and the distressed patient required a treatment so lengthy that, back in Physio once more, Tansy kept her clothes on and settled for an armchair in the staffroom and a triple-strength instant coffee. The armchair was lumpy and the coffee bitter, but its caffeine content kept her awake as intended. She tried to read, but her mind kept straying to the Isle of Mull, where Calum had returned to join his father's veterinary practice and—and this was the really distressing thing—to marry his childhood sweetheart.

Discovering that she'd been nothing but a stopgap, a convenience, had been devastating, because Tansy hadn't had an inkling that that was how it was. Apart from the hurt of losing the man she loved, Calum's deceit had destroyed her self-confidence. Now she trusted neither her intuition nor the integrity of any man she met. Presumably she would get over it some day—as Kirsty said, women did or else they went under—but when? Meanwhile, life was hardly any fun. Especially not now that her path had crossed with Struan McLeod's. Her only comfort was that Struan knew nothing of her affair with his brother.

Calum had taken care that she shouldn't meet his twin or any others of his family, and she'd sometimes wondered why. She had understood, though, when he had dumped her. Her existence had had to be kept a secret from Marie, the childhood sweetheart waiting patiently at home for Calum to finish his training and get some post-grad experience—and to sow his wild oats at her, Tansy's, expense!

But look, it was nearly six, and time to go and treat nice Mr McKenna again. What an ordeal he was having for a man in his seventies. And you think you've got troubles, Tansy Nicholson!

* * *

Tansy emerged from the shower as the first physios came trickling in for the day. Kirsty was one of them. 'Are you early or late?' she asked.

So guess who didn't go home at all last night, thought Tansy, smiling inwardly as she told her story to a sympathetic audience. But it was over now and she could afford to shrug it off. She ended philosophically with, 'All the luck of the draw, girls. It could be better next time.'

The first person she saw on the ward that morning was Sister Aitken. Who else? 'You look terrible, Miss Nicholson!' exclaimed Mighty Mouse severely.

'I know, Sister.'

'Are you ill?'

'No — thank you. Just tired. You see I — '

Sister interrupted her with a massive snort and launched into a tirade about girls who put their social lives before their patients. 'Now in *my* day,' she was saying when she was interrupted by Struan McLeod. He was also looking rather the worse for his night on duty, but Sister didn't rail at him. He was a man and a doctor. And then the neurologist appeared, intent on squeezing in his examination of Mrs Clarke before starting his clinic. Sister then switched on the nearest thing to sweetness she ever managed and fluttered after him to the patient's bedside.

Struan regarded Tansy with sympathy. 'No need to ask what that was all about,' he said. 'She really does go too far sometimes. Why did you not tell her what a heavy night you've had?'

'She never gave me the chance.'

'That sounds familiar. Mighty Mouth would be a better name for her. The other is nothing but an insult to an inoffensive wee beastie. Don't work too hard today,' he advised, before continuing up the corridor.

A kind thought, that, no matter how unlikely it was that she could act on it. Tansy decided then that if it weren't for his appearance and his identity there might be something to be said for Dr Struan McLeod.

She had to treat the chests first of all. They were all a little better except for Mrs Pringle. 'I don't think I could stand all that moving and pummelling today, hen,' she sighed. 'Could we not put off the therapy until I'm better?'

It was difficult to know how best to answer that! Fortunately the effort of speaking so forcefully had made Mrs Pringle cough, so Tansy seized the chance to clear the upper airways at least with a few well-directed vibrations to the chest wall. 'I'll have a word with the doctor,' she promised afterwards. 'If he says you needn't have postural drainage, then we'll leave it. Otherwise. . .'

Mrs Pringle nodded resignedly. 'I know. It's up wi' the foot of the bed and tail in the air.' She coughed again, shifting nothing this time. 'I'd not have your job for fifteen thousand a year,' she added soulfully.

I would, thought Tansy. With that kind of money I'd go straight to the nearest garage and buy a car! 'Would you like me to pour you an orange juice, Mrs Pringle?'

'Thanks, love.' Tansy held the glass while the patient drank, by which time a radiographer had trundled a portable X-ray machine to the foot of the bed. Tansy was glad. Now she'd know for sure whether the lower lobes of those lungs were as clogged-up as she suspected. She wasn't yet confident enough to trust to her stethoscope alone.

Mrs Baird was very cheerful today because last night her husband had said how peaceful the house seemed without his mother in it, grumbling all the time. Even the dog had noticed and was back to his preferred dozing place on the hearthrug. Her cheerfulness was reflected in her performance — two lengths of the ward without her stick, followed by half a flight of stairs for an encore.

Mrs Clarke was less happy. 'That nervous specialist who came earlier rolled me about something shocking,' she complained. 'I told him he could do with taking handling lessons from you, m'lass.'

And I'll bet that went over big with the hospital's senior neurologist, thought Tansy, while thanking her patient for the compliment. 'So you'll not mind if I give you a few more exercises today, then?' she assumed.

'Och away, ye're a crafty wee besom,' was the answer.

Sister had a meeting that morning and the cleaners were laying on quick cuppas in the kitchen for the nurses, to save them the long walk to the canteen for their mid-morning break, as regulations required. The canteen was miles away so more often than not they went without when they were busy. Tansy was included in this treatment and, chatting to a nursing colleague, she discovered that she wasn't the only victim of Sister's disapproval.

By then, Mrs Pringle's X-rays were hanging up on the viewing screen in the office, so Tansy went to look at them. She was making notes when Nemesis struck. 'And what do you think you're doing in here, Miss Nicholson?'

Making custard, of course, you silly old. . . 'Just looking at Mrs Pringle's latest X-rays, Sister. She *is* on my list.'

'And in my opinion, she is not well enough to withstand physio!'

So that was where Mrs P. got that idea, guessed Tansy.

'And I intend speaking to Dr McLeod about it when he. . . Oh, there you are, Doctor. Would you please come and look at these films?' Sister called out as Struan passed by the open door.

Obediently he checked and came in. 'Have *you* seen these, Miss Nicholson?' he asked after a careful scrutiny.

'Yes, Doctor.' And then, because he was regarding her quizzically, 'Mrs Pringle says she doesn't feel well enough for physio, but by the look of these——'

'She's in danger of drowning in her own secretions if she doesn't have it,' he finished for her decisively.

'But you've put her on antibiotics, Doctor,' bristled Sister.

'Which will gradually bring the infection under control, but do nothing to clear away the present copious secretions,' he explained patiently. Tansy got the feeling that this wasn't the first time they'd debated this point. 'Go to it, then,' he said to her, 'but use your discretion about length, frequency and intensity of treatment. The poor lady must be feeling quite ill.'

'Yes, I'll do that—thank you, Doctor.'

Tansy was about to leave when he asked how she was bearing up after her sleepless night. 'Miss Nicholson was on call last night and was kept constantly on the go,' he told Sister, winking at Tansy over Sister's head.

She felt a sudden rush of gratitude as she admitted to feeling very tired, but added that she hoped to survive. How kind of him to put Sister in the picture like that, especially when he was probably feeling none too bright himself, having also been on duty. Except, of course, that he'd had Staff Nurse Norton to succour him! Tansy thanked him all the same, getting another of those smiles that were so heartbreakingly like his brother's.

She discovered that frequent short treatments suited

Mrs Pringle best, so she was toing and froing for the rest of the day, in between her other tasks. By five o'clock, even the patient was ready to admit to breathing more easily. 'But I'm looking forward to a nice quiet evening,' she warned.

Tansy gently broke it to her that she must expect at least one visit later on from the duty physio. 'I'm afraid this is one of those times when it's a lot of what you don't fancy that does you good,' she said as she plumped up the pillows.

Mrs Pringle closed her eyes in resignation. 'I reckon you could talk an Arab into buying a sand-pit,' she sighed.

But not Calum into loving me, thought Tansy sadly as she went to collect the ice canister for humping down to Physio. If only he'd levelled with me! Then I could have weighed the pros and cons and when I lost out to Marie I'd only have had myself to blame. But not to say anything—and to let me think I was the one and only. . .

'No wonder you're looking so miserable,' said Struan McLeod. 'That thing must weigh a ton. Here, give it to me.' He took it from her and tucked it under his arm as though it weighed nothing.

'Careful, it might leak! Oh, dear, now your jacket's all wet. I *am* so sorry.'

'So am I, but it's not your fault.' He set the thing down on the corridor floor and mopped at the watery trickle on his well-cut Glenurquart tweed jacket with a snow-white handkerchief. Then he picked it up again, with both hands and right way up this time. 'You press the button,' he said when they reached the lift.

'But I thought staff weren't supposed to use the lift.'

'To hell with that,' said the senior registrar. 'Press the button.'

'Yes, Dr McLeod.'

'Do you mean to tell me that you tote this confounded thing up and down the stairs every day?' he asked as they whirred gently downwards.

'Yes, Doctor. We all do. Those of us who need ice in wards that don't have a supply, that is. Of course Surgical Neurology, where we use it most, has its own supply.'

'Can the porters not do it? Open the gate, then, lassie, we've arrived.'

'Oh, so we have — sorry. We tried that, but they couldn't always spare the time, so now we transport it ourselves. Anyway, it's not as heavy as a helpless patient. Thank you, Doctor, this is where I turn off.'

'I'm making for the car park and Physio is more or less on my route,' he insisted when she tried to take back the canister.

'You're awfully kind,' Tansy found herself saying for the second time that day.

'It's my speciality — especially when pretty girls are involved.'

That provoked Tansy's heaviest frown and Struan asked, puzzled, 'So what did I say? You're looking almost as forbidding as you did before I offered to carry this wretched thing.'

She could hardly tell him she had been frowning then because she had been thinking of his treacherous brother, and was frowning now because he was behaving exactly like him! 'It was the "pretty girl" bit,' she was prepared to admit. 'I don't go for — that sort of thing.'

'All right, I'll admit it was rather corny.' He regarded her with something like disappointment. 'You're not a feminist, by any chance?'

She certainly was not — just a naïve little idiot who

had thought his too charming brother meant all the things he'd said! But getting on the wrong side of Struan because Calum was a cad was pointless. 'Please ignore that,' she said with a tiny smile. 'I guess it's just that I'm plain exhausted.' They had reached Physio now and Tansy took back her ice canister at last. 'Thanks again. That was really kind and I'm very grateful.'

'No problem,' he said. 'But you are, you know.'

'I am — what?'

'Pretty. I was only telling the truth.' And before she could say anything, he walked on down the corridor towards the exit.

When Tansy's flatmate came into the changing-room, Tansy was staring earnestly at her reflection in the mirror above the wash-basins. 'Things *are* looking up,' said Kirsty. 'I haven't seen you so much as glance towards a mirror for months. What brought this on?'

'My skin is awful,' stated Tansy after a moment's thought.

'Your skin is flawless and well you know it. Sure, you're as white as snow just now, and there are great dark circles under your eyes, but that's only because you're whacked. The roses'll be back tomorrow after a good night's sleep.'

'And I'm sick of my hair.'

'Don't start all that again,' begged Kirsty, casting an envious glance over Tansy's straight and shining chest-nut bob. 'Believe me, you'd give your slender ankles for it if you were a washed-out blonde like me. Cheer up, for heaven's sake, and I'll do you something especially nice for your supper tonight.'

'But it's really my turn to cook,' said Tansy, as she pulled her tunic over her head.

'And if I let you in your present dozy state, you'll

probably fall asleep over the stove and set light to your hair. Then you'd really have something to complain about. Come on! If we hurry, we can get a lift with Geraldine. I just heard her say she's going to Safeway.'

Over lamb cutlets and cauliflower at the round pine table in the kitchen of their neat wee rented flat, Tansy and Kirsty were talking about Kirsty's spring wedding. It was increasingly the topic of conversation as the preparations got under way. 'Are you absolutely sure you don't mind wearing blue?' asked Kirsty, because blue was not a colour Tansy ever wore. It didn't seem to go with her dark brown eyes.

'Of course I don't mind—if it's got a hint of green in it. Besides, blue suits your wee sister so well.'

'But you're chief bridesmaid, so you really ought to have a say.'

'I don't mind, Kirsty—honestly. Now tell me, has Hamish decided who to have for his best man yet?'

'If he's not to fall out with his mother, he'll have to ask his brother, though he'd much rather have one of his medical pals.' Here Kirsty paused before continuing tentatively, 'Talking of whom, how are you getting on with Struan McLeod?'

Tansy considered that very tactless when Kirsty must be aware that he was Calum's twin, but she answered casually enough, 'Oh, all right, you know. But why do you ask? He's not one of Hamish's crowd, is he? He wasn't at your engagement party.'

'That was because he was working down in the Borders at the time.'

'I see—well, I can't pretend I'm sorry he wasn't there. He's too much like his brother for comfort.'

'Mmm.' Kirsty leaned earnestly forward across the table. 'That bastard hurt you very much—I know that—but it's more than six months now, since. . .' She gave a great sigh of frustration. 'Look, love, what I'm trying to say is, why not give life another chance? We could fix up a foursome one night soon. Hamish knows several really nice guys who're not seriously attached. Say yes, Tans—do!'

'I'm getting myself together again, really I am. But no contrived dates, please, Kirsty. I'd rather just—let things happen. If they're going to.'

'All right, then, so long as you do. Let things happen, that is. But the way that swine Calum treated you has knocked your confidence for six and now you seem unable to trust any man. But they're not all bastards, you know—far from it. OK, end of lecture.' Kirsty got up from the table and carried their plates over to the sink. 'I went really mad this evening and bought your favourite cheesecake. A slice of that with a cup of decaffeinated, and then it's off to bed with you, my cherub. And no argument!'

CHAPTER TWO

KIRSTY'S prediction was right. Tansy did feel better after a good night's sleep — and just as well, too, because on the way to the wards next morning Bill Cox broke the news that she would have to go on Dr Tait's ward round. 'You can't do this to me, Bill,' she wailed. 'I don't know a thing about your patients.'

'Sorry, hen, but this is an emergency. Because he's chairing a meeting at the international symposium this afternoon, Professor Carlisle is doing his round this morning instead. And as he's head of the unit, I must go round with him.'

'Dr Tait scares me to death.' Though not as much as Mighty Mouse. . . 'And as for Sister, she'll just chew me to bits.'

'She will not, because he'll not let her. Donald Tait is just about the only person who can keep her in check. See here, Tansy, I sat up half the night writing these copious notes about all my patients. All you have to do is read out the bits I've underlined.'

'Are you quite sure I can cope?' Tansy asked worriedly.

'Of course I'm sure. You only need to be there, answer his questions with the aid of these notes, and make a note of anything you hear which you think I should know.'

It sounded simple, but then so did almost anything if you knew how to put it. 'OK, then, but when will I do my work?'

'I'll give you a hand with your acute chests now and give you as much time as I can later on.'

Having put the first part of that programme into operation, Bill then went off to join the professor, after giving Tansy an encouraging pat on the shoulder and telling her not to worry, because he knew she'd do just fine. Tansy tacked on to the back of Dr Tait's retinue and wished she were invisible.

She wasn't, though. 'And where is Mr Cox?' demanded Sister as soon as she noticed.

Tansy opened her mouth to reply, just as Dr Tait said, 'It's all right, Sister, Bill has already explained, and I'm sure this charming young lady will be a splendid substitute.'

Anybody with half an eye could see that Sister was bursting to tell him just how wrong he was, but didn't quite dare. 'Cheer up, sweet maid. With any luck, she'll turn back into a frog any minute,' whispered Struan McLeod so close to Tansy's left ear that she could feel his warm breath on her neck. She hadn't realised he'd dropped to the back of the queue.

His proximity and his chumminess and the delightful picture he'd painted of Sister Aitken's transformation were altogether too much. Tansy let out a smothered laugh, turned it into a cough, couldn't find her hankie, and dropped her folder, sending Bill's carefully prepared notes fluttering in all directions.

'She has certainly made an excellent start,' remarked Sister with heavy sarcasm.

With the help of Struan and the sympathetic housewoman, the notes were soon gathered up. Tansy whispered her thanks, stuffed them back in the folder, and prepared to pay attention.

The first three patients were all new admissions for investigation, and nothing was required of Tansy but to listen and learn, just as though she were a student again. So far, a doddle.

But next on the list was Mr Lothian, a special patient of Bill's.

'X-rays, please, Sister,' said the consultant. He held them up to the light so that he and Struan could view them and confer. Tansy managed to get a glimpse too.

'Nothing there,' muttered Dr Tait. What did he mean? She had definitely spotted some early osteo-arthritic changes in the right hip.

'How's the physio going, Miss — er — er. . .?' Dr Tait barked suddenly.

'W — well. . .' Tansy scrabbled in the folder for the sheet headed 'Lothian'. 'Responding well,' she read out for starters.

'Ah'm no better and if anything I'm worse,' corrected the patient.

'So is Mr Cox being a trifle optimistic, then?' wondered Dr Tait.

Tansy stuck with it. 'Responding well,' she repeated. 'Pain definitely muscular in origin. Gynae reports negative. . .' Her voice petered out in dismay and her cheeks burst into flame.

The housewoman smothered a chuckle and Sister's eyebrows rose to the stratosphere. Struan calmly removed the folder from Tansy's trembling hands and opened it, while Dr Tait observed woodenly that Mr Lothian must be very relieved to know that his sexual identity was not in doubt.

Struan put another paper into Tansy's hands. 'There's also a *Mrs* Lothian in the ward, sir,' he explained matter-of-factly. But Tansy was now beyond speech, so he cupped her elbow in a reassuring way and read out over her shoulder, 'Connective tissue massage begun on Thursday the third of February. No obvious improvement noted yet, but the acute cutting sensation experienced by the patient during treatment suggests that he will eventually respond.'

'There we are, then, Mr Lothian,' said Dr Tait. 'These things take time, you know.' He then launched off into the whys and wherefores, while Tansy wilted back against Struan McLeod's solid substance, finding that wonderfully comforting until sanity returned. She straightened up then and forced her thoughts into the proper channels. No wonder they weren't bothered about those arthritic changes. It would have been sclerosing or hardening arteries they were looking for.

Struan had now got Bill's notes into order and he handed the folder back to Tansy. 'All shipshape now,' he whispered. 'And do try not to look so suicidal. It could have happened to anybody.'

Tansy signalled her gratitude with expressive brown eyes and got a friendly wink in exchange. That would have been comforting — if only it hadn't made him look more like Calum than ever.

She sighed audibly as Dr Tait asked, 'And how are you today, Mr Dewar?'

'Coming along just fine, thank you, Doctor. Yon wee lassie there is clearing my lungs a fair treat.'

'Yes, he's quite clear now, sir,' confirmed Struan. 'I think he could go home tomorrow.'

'Fine, fine. But lay off the tobacco in future, there's a good man. You might not be so lucky next time,' advised the consultant.

Nothing else disastrous occurred and Tansy actually collected some praise for the improvement in Mrs Baird's mobility. Emboldened, she thought of raising the question of the disruptive resident mother-in-law, but Struan was already stating the problem briefly but clearly, causing Dr Tait to nod his firm agreement. 'Have a word with the husband,' he authorised.

Tansy was very pleased to see that Struan's thoughtfulness extended to his patients as well as to his colleagues. Yes — but for his completely impossible family connections, there would be a lot to be said for Dr Struan McLeod.

It was customary to gather in the office for coffee and more discussion after ward rounds, but as the others filed in Tansy hung back. Struan paused in the doorway to smile encouragingly and wave her in. 'No, I mustn't,' she said. 'I'm all behind with my work.' Then the minute he was over the threshold, Sister clinched things by shutting the door in her face.

So endeth my first ward round as a qualified person, thought Tansy, as she scurried away to get on with her work. It had hardly been an unqualified success!

Bill Cox came looking for her soon afterwards. 'So how did it go?' he asked.

'Oh, Bill — it was awful! I dropped your notes and got them all mixed up and read out Mrs Lothian's report instead of Mr's, and now Dr Tait thinks I'm dreadfully dim.'

'If he does, then he's wrong, because you're not,' Bill returned firmly. 'Anyway, I can cap that. On my first ward round on Surgical Neurology, I managed to disconnect a catheter while trying to turn an unconscious patient, and squirted the prof with urine.'

'You didn't!' Tansy sounded horrified, but she was feeling better already.

'True as I'm standing here, so old Tait got off lightly, wouldn't you say?'

'You're such a tonic, Bill.'

'Stop looking at me like that, you wee hussy,' he

ordered, 'or I may forget I'm a married man. Want some help to make up for lost time?'

When Tansy went to see Mrs Pringle again that lady said, 'I know you're very busy today, dear, so I'll not mind if you give me a miss.'

'That's very kind of you, but I couldn't possibly do that,' said Tansy earnestly. 'You're my top priority.'

Mrs Pringle said that at any other time she'd be flattered. Then the effort of talking made her cough which, as Tansy gently pointed out, rather proved her point. She was improving, though — no doubt about that. So too were most of the other chests. Was it safe to hope that the flu epidemic was on the wane? She'd be lucky to get through all her treatments by Sister's deadline of patients' suppertime, though. 'Tea in the office at four, Tansy,' said the staff nurse gleefully, breaking in on Tansy's musings. 'Sister's just gone off for a long weekend and Mrs Pringle's given us the gooey chocolate cake her sister brought in because she's not feeling up to it.'

Tansy said she'd be there come hell or high water, but tea-parties behind Sister's back were quite forgotten when halfway through the afternoon they had an emergency admission. 'Young girl. Found collapsed in the street,' explained a nurse as she hurried by.

When the patient was wheeled in on a trolley, the ward doctor was with her. Tansy had to pass to get to her next patient and she wondered what was going on behind the drawn curtains. When choosing her career, she had been very torn between nursing and physiotherapy, and at times like this she was inclined to think she'd made the wrong choice. Physios are very useful, but nurses are vital, she was telling herself, when Struan burst into the ward and brushed past her without a glance in his haste to get to the patient. Doctors were vital too.

Tansy worked on steadily, making her useful but not vital contribution, and still those cubicle curtains remained drawn, while flying figures came and went.

She went to treat two of her male patients next, and when she returned to the female ward the curtains were still drawn.

All was now quiet. Very quiet. 'They lost her,' whispered Mrs Pringle. 'Nobody could say they didn't try, but she slipped away. Young Dr Findlay was almost in tears, the poor lassie. I had a bit of a weep myself. They say she couldn't have been more than thirty.'

What a waste, thought Tansy, feeling rather like weeping herself. Who had the girl left behind? A heart-broken husband? Children? But Mrs Pringle was coughing fruitily and Tansy's immediate duty was to relieve the congestion. 'It sounds to me as I've come at just the right moment for once,' she said gently.

'Aye,' breathed Mrs Pringle, taking Tansy's hand and holding on tight for a second, before turning on to her side, ready for treatment, without being asked.

Tansy had barely finished making her comfortable again afterwards when a nurse popped her head round the curtain to say, 'You're wanted on the office phone, Tansy. It's the finance department.'

'Thanks—I'll be there as soon as I can,' said Tansy. Mrs Pringle suggested she might be in for a rise. 'More likely a fine,' she quipped in return as she pulled back the curtains, noting at the same time that the cubicle where the battle for life had been fought and lost was now empty.

In the office, Struan and the junior registrar continued their earnest, low-voiced discussion while Tansy was taking her call. First came a curt request to be told who had authorised the taxis she had ordered in the early hours of Thursday morning.

'Well, nobody, I suppose,' she returned, frowning. 'I mean — I just thought that was what one did. Between the hours of eleven p.m. and seven a.m. Is that not right, then?'

'Yes, but only with authorisation,' said the disembodied voice. 'You should have submitted a slip signed by the doctor requesting the attendance. So I'm afraid you will be charged.' She was making it sound like a criminal matter.

'But really it was the other way round. That is, I had to stay on here later than expected, so I had to get a taxi home. Then, soon after, I was called in again, but that time I stayed here — if you see what I mean.'

'Sorry, but I don't,' said the voice. 'You'll be getting an invoice for seven pounds twenty.'

'Seven pounds twenty,' echoed Tansy, aghast.

'You should have stayed here all night,' reproved the voice.

'But I didn't know I would have to come back. And anyway, I was on call, not on stand-by. . .' Too late. Tansy was protesting to a dead line.

Struan must have overheard, because he broke off his discussion with Dr White to ask what all that had been about. Tansy explained, sounding suitably ill-used, and he told her not to worry, because he would sort it all out and see that the office got their precious bit of paper.

'I really don't know how to thank you — you're so kind,' she told him, sounding as though she'd just made an amazing discovery.

'Try buying me a beer some time,' he suggested with a grin, before saying to his junior with a complete change of mood, 'So there was no other means of identification, then, Pete?'

'No. None. Just the name on that crumpled envelope in her coat pocket. Gerda Malpas.'

Tansy froze in her tracks and turned slowly like somebody in a dream. They were—they had to be— talking of the girl who had died in the ward that afternoon. 'Excuse me,' she croaked in a voice that didn't sound like her own. 'But I know—knew her. I knew Gerda Malpas.'

'You did?' they exclaimed together.

'Not very well—just to speak to in the street. She was a neighbour.'

'Tell me everything you know,' Struan ordered urgently.

'It's not that much really. Just that she had a flat on the next stair to us on the other side of the park. Twenty-five Alexandra Terrace. She only moved in about three months ago and she's a single parent with two wee boys.' Tansy caught her breath. 'My God— those two poor babies. . .'

'Sit down, Tansy,' said Struan gently, drawing forward a chair and pushing her into it. 'This girl you know may not be our patient at all, but there's only one way to find out. Do you feel up to identifying her for us?'

Tansy swallowed hard. 'Yes, I'll—I'll do it. We never exchanged more than a few words when we met, but she told me her name herself.'

'That's good enough.' He straightened up and pulled Tansy to her feet. His grip was firm and immensely comforting.

They had put Gerda in an empty side-ward, and one glance was sufficient. Tansy nodded without speaking, her eyes filling with tears.

Without a word, Struan took her hand again and led her back to the office. By then the tears had overflowed and she was dabbing at them ineffectually with a paper tissue. Struan produced his handkerchief and offered it silently. His other arm was already firmly round her waist.

She thanked him wordlessly with a watery little smile which he answered by increasing the pressure of his arm. Unthinkingly, she leaned against him, and it was just as comforting as it had been that morning. But for every sort of reason, this simply wouldn't do. Tansy mopped up her tears and lifted her head from his shoulder, wondering what had possessed her to put it there in the first place. 'It's too bad of me to be giving way like this, but that was rather a shock,' she excused herself unsteadily. 'So yet again, I have to thank you for being so kind.'

Struan loosened his hold on her. 'Yes, it's astonishing how often I seem to give you cause to do that,' he returned thoughtfully. 'But what puzzles me is why you always sound so surprised. Why is that?'

How could she tell him it was because she found him more considerate than the brother he resembled? 'I think,' she began hesitantly, 'I think it's because, were I in your shoes, I'd be finding me rather a wimp. And a nuisance. So I'd be inclined to keep out of my way.'

Struan's glance was both knowing and disturbing. 'That can't be true, or it would mean you were selfish and uncaring. And if you were, you'd not be so upset about that poor girl.'

Somehow she had to put a stop to this probing, this intimacy. 'I was shocked,' she insisted. 'What happened to her, anyway?'

He accepted her drawing back with a scarcely perceptible shrug. 'She was found just around the corner from the hospital in a diabetic coma.'

'Undiagnosed?' Tansy asked quickly.

'We think it must have been, but why do you ask?'

'Because one day when we'd been talking together a bit longer than usual, she said she'd have to get on as she was dying to go to the loo. She said jokingly that she was never out of the place these days and what did I think was up? I told her it could be any of several things and the only way to find out was to see a doctor. She promised me she would as soon as she got settled in.'

'She mentioned no other symptoms? No excessive thirst, weight loss, pins and needles, sore throat?'

'No, nothing like that. If she had, I think I'd have guessed and told her she absolutely *must* see a doctor. I wonder why she didn't?'

'Perhaps she did, and then got careless about her insulin. It happens. But my guess is that if, as you said earlier, she really is alone, she kept putting it off because she was worried about what would happen to her children if she had to go into hospital. I know that sounds crazy, but, believe me, she's not the first mother to do that.'

'She was certainly devoted to her little ones. I wonder what will happen to them now? I could look after them over the weekend, but——'

'That doesn't sound much like the girl who would turn her back on other people's troubles,' Struan said gently. 'Not to worry, though. Now that we have her address, the police will fill in the background and try to trace any relatives. She's probably got parents some-where—brothers and sisters too, perhaps.' He looked at his watch. 'Anyway, it's getting late. You'll be wanting to get home and I've some loose ends in urgent

need of tying up.' His voice softened some more. 'I was
sorry to have to ask you to identify her, but it was very
helpful; not least for the sake of the children. Thank
you.'

'That's all right,' Tansy said awkwardly. 'I mean, one
does what one can. . .'

'Most of us do, anyway,' he agreed as he picked up
the phone.

All the way home, Tansy's thoughts were with
Gerda's little boys. Social workers, or, better still, some
relative would come to the rescue. Either way, they
would be cared for. But what must the poor wee things
be feeling? Tansy's own mother had died young and
she could still vividly recall her own bewilderment and
pain.

As this was Hamish's weekend off, Kirsty had gone
with him on a duty visit to his family, so Tansy had the
flat to herself. She put in a boring but necessary Friday
evening doing chores and went early to bed, so as to be
fresh for her work next morning.

When she walked into Physio, Bill Cox was already
there and making out the lists. Weekend work was
supposed to be limited to emergency treatments only,
but physios had their own opinions about leaving
patients two whole days without treatment and there
were always several of them there unofficially on
Saturdays to cope with their priorities. No prizes for
guessing that most of them will be chests today, thought
Tansy.

'Well, m'lass, what's it to be?' Bill asked cheerfully.
'Would you like ICU, Cardiac, Surgical or the nice
familiar ground of your own unit?'

'You mean you're giving me a choice?'

'Sure. There are three of you juniors on this morning and as you're the first to arrive. . .'

'Medical, please,' Tansy chose hurriedly as the other two came buzzing in.

'I wish I'd had a tenner on that,' laughed Bill as he handed over the appropriate records.

He had thoughtfully starred those patients who might need two visits, and, as one was Mrs Pringle, Tansy began with her.

'Have you not heard of the five-day week?' sighed that lady when she opened her eyes to see Tansy at her bedside.

'I have, but the microbes haven't,' Tansy answered bracingly. 'You should feel honoured, Mrs P. Not everybody gets a going-over on Saturdays, you know.'

Mrs Pringle said that if there were any honours going, then she'd rather have the OBE, and Tansy promised to have a word with Buckingham Palace if Mrs P. would just be a darling and turn on her side right now. During her treatment, Tansy could hear Struan's soft West Coast voice as he talked to the patient in the next bed, but by the time she'd finished he'd left the ward.

'I s'pose you'll be coming back later,' said Mrs Pringle doubtfully. 'So who else is getting the honour, then?' she asked when Tansy had told her yes, but, as she was so much better, she might escape with just a check.

'Mrs Jardine and three of the men,' said Tansy.

'So you'll be getting off early then this morning, dear.'

Tansy said, 'Anything but.' Ward Eighteen was only the beginning; she was covering the whole unit this morning.

Mr Barrie had been smoking again. He denied it, of course, but the acrid smell was a dead give-away to the

sensitive nostrils of a non-smoker. Tansy read the riot
act as firmly as her lowly rank allowed and threatened
him with Sister Aitken if he didn't behave.

'Not only smokers get bad chests,' he argued.

'That's true, but you get them more,' said Tansy,
holding ungrammatically to her point. Mr Barrie sent
her on her way with the news that she was 'a terrible
wumman'.

One of the patients for treatment in Ward Twenty
was nice Mr McKenna who had needed so much
attention on Wednesday night. He was off the ventilator now and feeling just grand, he insisted. Tansy
thought that unlikely, but silently applauded his spirit
as she clapped and vibrated his chest to loosen the
secretions still clogging up his airways.

It was getting on for noon by the time she returned
to her own ward to do her last two treatments. She
hadn't seen Struan McLeod all morning, which was
something of a disappointment. Last night before she
had gone to sleep, Tansy had done some hard thinking.
While Struan was virtually indistinguishable in appearance from his twin, that didn't necessarily mean that
their personalities were identical. Calum might have
treated her badly, but Struan didn't know that. Therefore, to be hostile towards him when he had shown her
nothing but kindness was neither sensible nor fair.
From now on, she meant to be as nice to him as to any
other colleague — and, being Tansy, she couldn't wait
to start. And who knows? she thought, flying off into
the realms of fantasy. He might tell Calum about this
perfectly delightful physio at the Alex, and then Calum
might feel a pang or two about what he's thrown
away. . . Well, stranger things had happened.

Tansy was able to leave Mrs Pringle happy, having
told her one more visit that afternoon from the duty

physio was probably all she would need. As she passed the open door of the office on her way out, Staff called her in for a coffee. 'If you'd like one,' she added.

Tansy said it was just what she needed, and inside she found Struan and Dr Findlay, the house physician.

'If only Sister could see us now,' said Mollie Findlay with a grin when they were all sitting down with a steaming mug apiece. 'I wonder what she'd say?'

'Nothing,' said Struan positively. 'She'd be too busy bursting into flame.'

Laughter seldom heard in that place bubbled round the little room, and they chatted on for a bit, agreeing what a shame it was that such a good and conscientious nurse was also so harsh in her dealings with colleagues. Then Staff said she'd better see if the lunches had appeared yet, and Mollie remembered she had a new admission to write up.

'And no doubt you have something urgent to attend to as well, Miss Tansy Nicholson,' supposed Struan provocatively when he and Tansy were alone. There was a challenge in his deep-set, smoky blue eyes which both excited and alarmed her.

'I'll certainly go if you think I should,' she answered breathlessly, 'but I've not finished my coffee yet.'

'Feel free to drink it as slowly as you like.'

'Thank you, Doctor. It shouldn't take me very long.'

'What a pity,' he said pointedly, and it could have been Calum speaking.

Tansy knew a painful jolt. 'I wonder why?' she just managed to reply in like vein before the phone rang.

'Blast!' said Struan emphatically as he picked it up.

Tansy finished her coffee as she waited quietly for the call to end. 'I have to go,' he said then, already on his feet and dalliance forgotten. 'See you.'

'Almost sure to,' she responded to his departing back

view. What a good thing that phone rang when it did, she thought. He's always been nice to me, but today he was definitely disposed to flirt.

Fifteen minutes later, Tansy was on a bus headed for Princes Street. She was going home for the rest of the weekend, but first she planned a snack lunch in Jenner's and a stroll round that wonderful department store. Immediate plans accomplished, she was waiting, later still, outside the store to cross over the road to Waverley station. Idly she surveyed the traffic, stiffening at the sight of Struan at the wheel of a Volkswagen and also waiting for the lights to change. Sitting beside him was the night staff nurse from Twenty. They were conversing with great animation, like two people who knew each other very well indeed.

Well, I'm damned, Tansy thought. He already has a girlfriend, yet he was chatting me up not two hours since. I'll not be worrying again about misjudging you, m'lad. There's nothing to choose between you and that honey-tongued, double-dealing brother of yours!

CHAPTER THREE

'FOR once, I am positively looking forward to work tomorrow,' announced Kirsty over hot chocolate at midnight on Sunday. 'Two whole days of Hamish's mother has depressed me. How she ever produced my fun-loving darling I cannot imagine.'

'I expect his nice father had something to do with it,' observed Tansy abstractedly. Her own weekend had not been completely carefree. Both her father and his sister who kept house for him had been looking very tired. And she'd also been thinking a lot about Gerda and her little boys.

'OK, so who are you fretting over now?' asked Kirsty, noticing.

Her family worries being too nebulous to define, Tansy told her about their next-door neighbour. 'If only I'd urged her more strongly that day to go to a doctor, she might still be alive,' she ended.

Kirsty said it was easy to think such things with hindsight, and that Tansy had done what was right at the time. As for the children, she'd met Mrs Smith from next door as she was coming in just now and Mrs Smith had told her that a very concerned granny had come up from Manchester, meaning to take them to live with her, once all the formalities were completed.

'Yes, but——' Tansy began but Kirsty cut her short.

'You worry too much about other people,' she insisted. 'If you put half as much energy into sorting out your own life, you'd be a lot happier.'

'I dare say you're right, but we are what we are,' returned Tansy. 'Oh, hell! I'm away to my bed now.'

At work next day, new patients and new problems had superseded Friday's tragic incident. As Staff remarked as she and Tansy climbed the stairs together, coping with a new emergency fairly stopped you brooding about the one before. 'And you'll have your work cut out today, Tansy. We've two new strokes in — and both still unconscious.'

'You're late, Miss Nicholson,' said Sister starchily from her throne behind the desk at her office.

Only about a minute and a half, but late was late in her book. Tansy looked pointedly at her watch. 'Yes, I believe I may be, Sister. I'm told there are some new cases for me.'

Sister swept an impatient hand over the two referral cards on the desk, wafting them on to the floor. Tansy bent down to retrieve them. 'And the case notes, Sister — '

'Dr McLeod has them in the doctors' room. And he is very busy.'

Translated, that meant, and don't you be running after him, you flighty wee besom. She needn't have worried. Tansy had no intention of pursuing Calum's twin.

However, his intentions were another matter. 'Hi there, Tansy,' she heard him call as she headed for the women's ward. 'About those strokes.'

Tansy turned and waited for him to catch up with her.

'Nice weekend?' he asked, smiling down on her.

'Very nice indeed, thanks,' she insisted. And then, with a superior little smile, 'What about you?'

'I was on duty,' he said, contriving to sound pathetic. 'Things were hectic. I hardly got time to breathe.'

But you squeezed in a trip to town with Staff Norton, she would have liked to remind him. 'Oh, dear—what a shame,' she said. 'But I'm sure you'll make up for it next weekend. You were going to tell me about my new patients, Doctor,' she reminded him as Sister sailed by, frowning.

'That's right, so I was.' Had he really forgotten? 'Let's see, now. The boss really wanted them in for investigation, since neither is typical. Mrs Strang has a left-sided paresis, but, contrary to the norm, her leg is more affected than her arm. Miss Alford's arm is not affected at all—only her leg. Does that suggest anything to you?'

'Trouble in the anterior cerebral artery, rather than the internal capsule,' said Tansy.

His eyes gleamed appreciatively. 'I say! Pretty *and* knowledgeable. Ten out of ten, that girl.'

Tansy might be wise to him, thanks to that chance sighting on Saturday, but she still intended to be pleasant. 'Just one of the little snippets of information I keep stashed away in my memory bank,' she said carelessly, 'but I am rather puzzled. I'm sure that Staff told me my two new stroke patients were unconscious, so how come —— ?'

'No wonder you're looking so perplexed,' said Struan McLeod. 'She obviously meant the two emergencies and I was talking of the two patients I want you to start on rehab right away. We've been talking at cross-purposes, Tansy.' He grinned at her and suggested slyly, 'Let's try to avoid that in future, shall we? I expect the other two will require routine chest care and positioning, but I'd like to check them over again first. All clear now?'

'Perfectly, thank you, Dr McLeod.'

'My friends call me Struan,' he invited.

'And why not?' Tansy asked casually. 'But I couldn't possibly. Sister Aitken already suspects me of running after you.'

'Sister Aitken suspects every female under fifty of running after me.' He grinned impishly again before saying, 'But in this case, I wouldn't exactly mind if she was right.'

'I bet you say that to all the girls,' Tansy retorted, retreating at great speed when Mighty Mouse sailed over the horizon again. Yes, he's definitely another Calum, she decided. Even to the quality of his repartee.

Bill had been reading the case-notes of the two unconscious stroke patients. 'You're going to have your work cut out,' he observed when they met a second later, 'so I'll take on the two newest ones and pass them on to you if they want to practise discrimination when they wake up.' Some of the older women didn't like the idea of a male therapist and Bill broad-mindedly met their wishes when it was possible. 'As for the other two, get them assessed this morning if you can and we'll discuss their treatment over lunch.'

'Thanks very much, Bill — I appreciate that, and I'll see them as soon as I've done my chests.'

Mrs Pringle was bubbling over with the news of her first visit to the toilet. 'Such a simple thing, but what a joy after trying to balance on those wretched bedpans. I swear I'm not the right shape for it.'

'Almost nobody is,' said Tansy. 'Our tutors were always grumbling that they ought to come in different sizes. But first things first. How's your chest today?'

'There's hardly anything coming up now and Dr Findlay thinks I'm just about clear.'

'All the same. . .' said Tansy, advancing with determination.

'I knew you'd say that! Some folk are never satisfied.'

Mrs Clarke's bed was now occupied by Miss Alford, one of the new stroke patients. She explained that she'd been told by one of the cleaners that Mrs Clarke had been transferred to Neurology with a diagnosis of collapsing leg nerves. 'Well, I'm glad to know where she's gone,' said Tansy, while doubting that diagnosis. 'I expect you've guessed that I'm the physiotherapist, Miss Alford. My name is Tansy Nicholson and, as I'm here, I may as well give you the once-over if you don't mind.'

'I was rather hoping I'd get that handsome young man who was in the ward a moment ago,' said the patient, discriminating positively in a way which Bill would appreciate. 'But as long as you know your stuff, I'll not complain.'

'You don't leave much to chance, do you?' she asked when Tansy had finished her questioning and measuring and feeling and otherwise testing the affected side. 'I suppose this blasted leg of mine will come right?'

'Given time, Miss Alford, but nerves can't be hurried, so you mustn't lose heart.'

'I'll not if you don't,' said the patient. 'Is that it for now, then? Right!' She picked up her newspaper to get on with the crossword.

What an interesting person, thought Tansy, going in search of her other new patient.

Mrs Strang was almost another Mrs Baird, both in her physical and her domestic problems. 'It's not that I don't like the awkward old devil,' she said of her father-in-law. 'Just that he's always exactly where I need to Hoover.'

'You'll not have been doing much Hoovering lately, though, Mrs Strang.'

'Och, no, my daughter's been doing everything before and after school. She's doing sixth-year studies and hoping to be a policewoman. She says the same, though. "Grandad's that bloody nosy, Mum. He's like a——"'

'Yes, they can be difficult,' agreed Tansy, gently but firmly staking her claim to a share of this conversation. 'But tell me. Have you ever had anything like this the matter with you before?'

It was difficult keeping Mrs Strang to the point, but eventually Tansy managed to complete her assessment. A short treatment came next, directed to her main problem of tight hamstrings. Then Tansy introduced her to Mrs Baird, because it was always a good idea to let a new patient see what could be achieved. And in this case the two of them could always fall back on their respective in-laws for a topic, when tired of talking ailments.

New patients meant being even more pressed for time than usual, so Tansy was very late going to lunch. From opposite directions, she and Struan McLeod arrived at the canteen together. 'Well timed,' he said, smiling into her eyes and reinforcing her opinion of him.

'Why?' she asked smartly. 'Are they closing up in a minute?'

'Oh, very witty. All the same, I have this funny feeling that you know perfectly well what I meant,' he whispered as they tacked on to the end of the queue.

'Perhaps I do and perhaps I don't,' she returned, 'but I'm lunching with Bill Cox, so that he can help me plan treatment for my new patients.'

'Lucky Bill Cox,' considered Struan McLeod. 'But tell me. Does this happen every day?'

'Oh, no—only when we've things to discuss.'

'And will you have things to discuss tomorrow?'

'That depends on whether you give me any more new and complicated patients, Doctor.'

'So the ball's in my court, then, is it?' he asked softly just as the assistant behind the servery roared, 'Next!'

Nothing would come of it, of course—why couldn't somebody *possible* be taking an interest in her?—but all the same, she had quite enjoyed that exchange. If nothing else, Calum's twin brother was providing her with the chance to polish up her sparring technique, which had been wilting from disuse.

Tansy returned to the ward after lunch armed with several new ideas for treatment, thanks to her discussion with Bill. In fact she devoted so much time to her stroke patients that she overran with her final chest treatments of the day and walked straight into Sister Aitken, who was presiding over the supper trolley.

But before Mighty Mouse could open fire, Struan materialised as if by magic. 'Still here, Miss Nicholson?' he asked. 'What a conscientious young person you are. Very praiseworthy, wouldn't you say, Sister?' he challenged.

'Her work seems all right—so far,' she allowed grudgingly. 'But you'll need to speed up a bit,' she told Tansy. 'Wait, please, Doctor. I want to speak to you,' Tansy heard next minute, confirming her suspicion that Struan meant to follow her.

He's certainly got his share of nerve, she thought, but then he doesn't know I spotted him with his girlfriend last Saturday. Shall I tell him or not? It would be interesting to see how he reacted. . .

'And what are you smirking about?' asked Kirsty when Tansy joined her in the changing-room.

'I didn't know I was,' protested Tansy. 'Anyway, it was nothing.'

'Oh, very convincing,' said her friend, 'but I can take a hint. Mind your own business, Kirsty Faulds. Right?'

'If you must know, I was rather amused at the way one of the ward doctors spiked Sister's guns when she set out to sink me for not getting finished on time.'

'That's nice to hear,' applauded Kirsty, 'but why could you not have said so in the first place?' Tansy hadn't decided how to answer that when Kirsty rushed on, asking, 'What's for supper tonight, Tans? And will there be enough for Hamish too?'

'Now she tells me,' wailed Tansy. The housekeeping money was getting low and she'd intended to economise with macaroni cheese. 'You'd better go on ahead,' she decided. 'I'm needing to go to the shops.'

A row of small shops across the road from the Alex did a roaring trade with the hospital staff, and as Tansy entered the butcher's Struan was coming out. 'So who's the lucky guy you'll be cooking for tonight?' he asked whimsically.

'Now there's a chauvinistic remark if ever I heard one,' she answered. 'Why should it not be the other way round?' Then she looked pointedly at his purchases. 'It looks to me as if some lucky girl is getting her dinner cooked by you tonight.'

His handsome face took on a soulful, nobody-understands-me look. 'It so happens that my young sister is visiting me this evening,' he informed her firmly.

That would be the youngest McLeod—a final-year architectural student, if Tansy remembered right. 'Lucky old you, having a sister. Actually, I'm an only child,' she added testingly. 'It must be great to have — brothers and sisters. . .'

'They can be a mixed blessing,' Struan stated positively.

Tansy hadn't expected that. 'Is she a bother to you, then?' she asked curiously.

Struan cocked an eyebrow as he asked, 'Whatever gave you that idea? But here she comes now,' he added as a jolly-looking girl came beaming into the shop toting a string bag full of vegetables. 'Tansy, meet my sister, Catriona. Catriona, Tansy Nicholson. We work together.'

They chatted amiably for a few minutes, but Tansy's mind wasn't wholly with the conversation, although she kept her side of it going well enough until Catriona pointed out that if Tansy didn't hurry she'd not get her meat before the butcher shut up shop.

Tansy thought about that encounter all the way home. She knew there were only three of them — the twins and the girl. So if Catriona wasn't the one who was a mixed blessing to Struan, then it had to be Calum. Yet she'd always imagined that identical twins saw eye to eye in everything. How strange.

Mrs Pringle was taking only a fraction of the time she needed this time last week, and she was so eager for therapy now. With no other really bad chests in the ward, Tansy was hoping to do one of her new stroke cases before elevenses — though 'tenses' would be more accurate when all mealtimes were that much earlier than the norm in hospital.

Miss Alford was a real handful. Not that she wasn't co-operative; she just insisted on knowing the purpose of every exercise and technique Tansy used. It was just like taking an exam. After treatment, when the patient declared herself completely exhausted, Tansy told her truthfully that she knew exactly how she felt.

In her way, Mrs Strang was also a handful, though in her case the problem was to slip in the instructions during her pauses for breath.

'Would you like a man for a change?' wondered Bill about halfway through the morning.

'Provided he's not too much of a talker,' Tansy answered with feeling.

Bill said that, on the contrary, Mr Buckie was rather withdrawn and Dr McLeod had suggested that she would be able to draw him out if anybody could. 'I think you've made a conquest there, Tansy, so go to it, lassie. He's a really nice guy.'

Tansy felt herself going pink, which made her very cross. 'Nonsense, Bill!' she denied fiercely. 'Anyway, he's got a girlfriend already.'

Bill chuckled before asking when any red-blooded man had ever let that stop him, to which Tansy replied crisply that if men played fair, then life would be a lot easier for women.

'This is getting a bit too deep for me,' said Bill, who knew nothing of the Calum episode. 'Now come and meet Tam Buckie. I'm sure you'll be good for him.'

The man had certainly got something to be depressed about, decided Tansy, after reading his notes. A promising young golf professional who found his legs going weak before he was halfway round the course? Of course he had.

When she introduced herself and told him why she had come, he looked at her without interest and said, 'All right,' then went back to staring at the ceiling. Initial testing showed normal strength for his age and general fitness level. 'So, then, this is a problem of endurance, rather than actual muscle power, Mr Buckie,' Tansy summed up at the end of his assessment.

'I'm not needing you to tell me that,' he returned shortly.

The lunches were now being given out, so Tansy said that she would discuss her findings with her colleague, Mr Cox, and plot a treatment programme for him.

She met Struan McLeod outside the canteen again and suspected that was more by design on his part than by accident. 'Well, fancy seeing you here,' she said lightly.

'There's nothing fanciful about it,' he retorted. 'With clinics both morning and afternoon today, this is our only chance to talk patients.'

'Sorry,' she said, 'but I really can't have lunch with you. Nobody would believe we were talking shop and I'm not aiming to be a subject for gossip.'

'Neither am I,' said Struan. 'That's why we're going over the road to Franco's. Come on!' He seized her arm and hurried her along.

'You're OK,' she said, noting that he had discarded his white coat for a Barbour jacket. 'But I could freeze to death outside in this weather.'

'So why do you think we're going round by Physio?' he asked patiently. 'Go in and get your coat.'

But when they were seated opposite one another in the snug seclusion of a café booth, Struan was in no hurry to begin the professional discussion he had suggested. Having ordered lasagne verde with side-salads, he planted his elbows on the table and regarded her steadily, his chin in his hands.

'Are you waiting for me to sing, or explode, or what?' asked Tansy after several pulse-raising seconds of this scrutiny.

'I was admiring you,' he returned in a caressing voice.

Such frankness was more or less guaranteed to disarm a girl. 'Er—thank you,' said Tansy, her repartee having deserted her.

'You're welcome,' said Struan, continuing to stare.

Tansy watched some newcomers taking their seats while she recovered. 'Mr Buckie,' she said then, firmly reminding him of the reason for this lunch.

'The name is Struan, actually.'

Tansy ignored that and battled on. 'I find him very interesting.'

'I hope I know how to take that,' warned Struan as the waitress deposited their food on the table. 'This looks rather better than the canteen nosh, don't you think?'

'Much better—but then that wouldn't be difficult. Does anybody have an idea about diagnosis?'

'How about sheer incompetence on the part of the cook?' he suggested. 'All right, all right—I give in,' he sighed, when she gave a gasp of exasperation. 'As it's definitely not MS, I suppose the most likely diagnosis in a man of Tam Buckie's age is polyneuropathy of unknown origin—if you can call that a diagnosis. We'll just have to wait until all his test results are back. He only came in on Sunday and yesterday was the first time I'd examined him.'

'Lumbar puncture?'

'Naturally—and a full blood count,' he told her between mouthfuls. 'And the senior reg from Neurology will be doing EMGs and nerve conduction-velocity tests this afternoon. If all that tells us nothing, then we'll have to consider a muscle biopsy. Eat up, Tansy. This is too good to waste.'

She obeyed for several minutes before asking doubtfully, 'I suppose there couldn't be a psychological element?'

He looked surprised. 'You mean, with Tam Buckie? There's always the chance, of course, but why? He seems to have everything going for him. He's certainly a bit depressed at the moment, but that's only to be expected.'

'Yes, that must be it. It's just that he seems so. . .' Tansy hesitated. 'Oh, I don't know how to put it — and I'm probably mistaken anyway.'

'Why should you be? After all, you women have a tremendous advantage over us mere males when it comes to such things.'

'In what respect?' she asked, genuinely puzzled.

'The famous feminine intuition, of course.'

Tansy positively snorted at that. 'Some of us have it, but more of us have not. And I'm definitely one of the have nots.'

'There's a story in there somewhere,' guessed Struan.

So there was, but not one for his ears. 'This lasagne is really super,' said Tansy.

'I wondered when you'd notice that,' he returned slyly. Oh, yes, Struan McLeod knew just as much about women as his brother.

He tried to persuade her to ice-cream and coffee, but Tansy had been watching the clock. 'I never allow myself the full hour for lunch,' she said. 'If I did, I'd never get through my work. But I enjoyed that — I really did. Thank you for thinking of it.' She was fumbling in her tunic pocket for her purse, but Struan had paid the bill before she produced a crumpled five-pound note. 'Please, you really must take this,' she urged, but he ignored it.

'I never allow a girl to pay on a date.'

'But that wasn't a date,' she protested when they had

managed to get across the busy road and back to the hospital gates. 'It was a discussion about patients. You said so yourself.'

'Don't tell me you really believe that was why I asked you.' He smiled.

'Why wouldn't I, Doctor?' she asked calmly.

'All right, have it your way,' he allowed as they reached Physio. 'So when *will* it be, then?'

'What?'

'That first date I thought we'd just had.'

'I shall have to think very carefully about that, Doctor McLeod,' returned Tansy for the benefit of two of her colleagues who happened to be passing.

As the week wore on, it appeared that Struan was also giving the matter some of that serious thought Tansy had claimed was needed. Not only did he not refer to it, but he had very little to say about anything else either. In fact he was so much less in evidence that Tansy decided he'd thought better of it and was deliberately keeping out of her way.

She told herself she ought to be grateful. The natural pleasure she'd felt at being noticed by an attractive man was cancelled out by the pain of being constantly reminded of his faithless brother. She'd have had to turn down any invitation of Struan's, so it would be less embarrassing for them both if he didn't repeat it.

This was Friday morning just before Dr Tait's ward round, and Tansy was handing over to Bill the progress reports on her patients, which she had sat up late the night before to prepare.

'You've included everything but mother's maiden name and favourite colour,' he commented humorously after scanning them. 'What a conscientious wee thing you are. I'll be hard put to it to do you justice in your end-of-placement report.'

'But I'm sure you'll do your best,' she told him confidently as they parted.

She had to see last weekend's two emergency admissions first, both now conscious and trying to come to terms with waking up, disabled, in hospital. Tansy did her best to cheer them by playing down difficulties and making much of every sign of improvement, however slight. 'These things take months, not weeks,' she repeated so often that she began to think she must sound like a parrot.

At least Mrs Baird was happy. Struan's talk with her husband had resulted in his sister agreeing to take their mother turn and turn about.

Mrs Strang was very envious. 'I wish I had a sister-in-law to share my problem,' she sighed, 'but the old divil only managed it the once and my husband's an only.'

Mrs Pringle was looking very chic in her best skirt and sweater as she waited to be discharged on the round. 'I'm sorry I was so difficult, dear,' she apologised, 'but some days I felt that ill ——'

'Of course you did and I knew that. If all my patients were as nice as you, I'd have a wonderful life,' insisted Tansy.

So it was compliments all round as they said goodbye and Mrs Pringle pushed a small box of chocolates into Tansy's pocket.

Once the ward-round procession appeared in the women's ward, Tansy slipped quietly out to go and work on the men. She had hoped to sneak a look at Tam Buckie's lab reports before the round, but Sister had been guarding the trolley. So when he asked her if she'd heard anything, she had to say no. 'But why did you not ask Dr Tait just now?' she wondered.

'Oh, you must know how it is,' he answered bitterly. 'The patient is always the last to get to know.'

'I'm sure you'll be told as soon as the diagnosis is made,' Tansy said bracingly. 'Perhaps there are still some reports yet to come in.'

'I should have been playing in Spain this week.'

Tansy could only murmur in sympathy, 'I'm sure we'll have you on the mend by spring.'

'That's no comfort,' he growled gloomily.

Why not? There was definitely something behind all this and she hadn't made much of a job of drawing him out so far. 'Taking the gloomy view all the time is not going to help,' she ventured gently.

'I'm beginning to think that nothing can help me,' said the patient, flinging himself flat on his back and staring up at the ceiling.

Nothing Tansy did or said that morning could persuade him to let her treat him, and she had to give up. It's almost as if he doesn't want to recover, she mused.

She was even more puzzled a little later on while having a quick cuppa in the kitchen with Staff, Sister being safely shut up in the office with the doctors. 'So all Tam Buckie's tests are negative, then,' said Staff.

'But he told me he hadn't heard anything!' exclaimed Tansy.

'I s'pose it's possible they haven't told him,' said Staff, 'but they usually do — as soon as they know.'

'So the mystery deepens,' returned Tansy thoughtfully as she washed her mug under the tap before going back to work.

'Are you the physio?' The afternoon was nearly over now and Tansy looked up from contemplation of Mr

Fraser's latest sputum sample to see a bluff, impatient-looking man peering round the cubicle curtain.

'I'm one of them, yes,' said Tansy coolly. 'Why do you ask?'

'If you're the one treatin' my lad, Tam Buckie, then I'd like a word.'

'Certainly, but, as you can see, I'm in the middle of a treatment here, so would you mind waiting outside for a few minutes?'

'I'm sorry for that lad,' said Mr Fraser when Buckie senior had reluctantly retreated. 'That auld yin's at him all the time to pull himself together and get going. I reckon he needs that sort of aggro like a hole in the heid.'

After ten minutes with the old man, Tansy was in whole-hearted agreement with that. Especially when she saw that Tam junior was looking even more depressed than usual. 'I suppose there's no chance of getting him banned, is there?' he asked pitifully. 'I can't take much more of his hassle. It's been the same all my life. "Dinnae mind the homework, son. You get out on the range and practise your swing." Never having made it to the top himself, he's hell-bent on making sure that I do. Bloody golf! I've lived with it all my life and. . .' He stopped suddenly, his facial muscles working.

It was obvious that he regretted that outburst, but it had been very enlightening. 'He pushed you into it as a career, didn't he?' Tansy prompted gently.

He nodded. 'I love the game really—but only as a game. I'll never be good enough to get to the top, but he'll not believe it. And now—this illness, whatever it is. . . He carries on as if it was all my own fault.'

So was this mysterious disease of his pathological or a physical expression of his frustration and inner turmoil? One thing was certain. She was the only member of staff he'd spoken to this frankly and the sooner she reported this conversation to a doctor, the better.

The first one she saw was Peter White, the junior registrar, and he was congratulating her when Struan came into the doctors' room. 'So what has Wonder Woman done now?' he asked, smiling down into her eyes and making her quite dizzy—contrary to common sense.

'Made the breakthrough with Tam Buckie, that's what. Go on, tell him, Tansy.'

Tansy got herself together and repeated her story, earning more congratulation. 'What he's told you confirms the psychological element,' said Struan. 'Now comes the difficult bit of getting him to acknowledge it. And yes, I agree that the father must be barred from visiting, now that we know he's the main cause of the problem.'

'How will you manage that?' wondered Tansy. 'He's a very determined old man.'

'The boss will think of something,' Struan said confidently. He turned to his junior. 'And if you were to dash down to Outpatients now, Pete, I think you'd catch him.'

'Sure, Struan, I can take a hint,' laughed Pete, neatly dodging the screwed-up memo Struan pitched at him.

Struan turned to Tansy the minute they were alone and his eyes were warm. 'It's been such a busy week,' he said.

'Yes, hasn't it? I'm really looking forward to the weekend.' Not the wisest of comments, Tansy, if you really want to keep off the subject of dates and leisure.

'Are you doing anything special?' he asked predictably.

Tansy invented a party for Saturday night.

'Given by anybody I might know?' Struan asked hopefully.

'I shouldn't think so. It's over in Fife.' That was where the Young Farmers' Club always had a knees-up on a Saturday, so it didn't have to be a lie.

'And what about Sunday?'

'I . . . We — haven't decided.'

'How do you like the sound of a walk over the Pentland hills, weather permitting, followed by high tea at the Flotterstone Inn?'

The truthful answer was very much indeed — if only you were almost anybody else! 'Sorry, but that's quite impossible,' she answered quickly. Too quickly.

Struan was frowning. 'To go walking at all — or to go walking with me?'

She dodged that by repeating that she would be away.

'And of course you couldn't possibly come back for Sunday, even if you wanted to. Which you don't.'

'I didn't say that ——'

'You didn't need to; I got the message. Are you always this indignant when a man asks you out?'

Indignant? Was that really how she'd sounded. 'Look, I'm very sorry, but. . . Actually, there is somebody. . .' She tailed off feebly, having dredged up the age-old excuse.

Struan's glance was cool now. 'In that case, it would have made more sense to turn me down after we had lunch on Tuesday.' The cool glance became a sneer. 'But that wouldn't have fed your ego quite so well, would it?'

He'd minded; and more than she'd thought he would. Tansy listened to his retreating footsteps and realised she had dented his pride as well as losing his goodwill.

She was also realising how much she regretted that,

but what else could she have done? He was Calum's brother, which made the whole thing impossible on two counts. Calum's identical twin wasn't likely to be any more reliable than Calum himself. Neither would Calum's twin be anything other than furious if he should find out he was a substitute. Because that was surely how he would see it. It was how she would have seen it herself. What other way was there of looking at it?

CHAPTER FOUR

TANSY was wondering what to wear. Initially, she'd intended making good her lie to Struan by going home to Fife again this weekend, but a heavy fall of snow overnight had scotched that idea. So instead, she was going to a party with Kirsty and Hamish.

She knew exactly how it would be. Crowds of folk she knew slightly or not at all would be milling about, too many getting drunk, and all feverishly pretending to be having the time of their lives, whether they were or not. Heavens, that was cynical! What was the matter with her? It wasn't very long since a Saturday-night party had represented the pinnacle of social success. 'I'll wear my black silk skirt and striped emerald blouse,' she decided aloud. It would probably turn out to be far too grand an outfit, but she felt good in it, and these days it wasn't getting nearly enough airings to justify its cost.

'You look far too grand for a rave-up in a tenement,' said Kirsty when both girls were ready. 'I thought you'd be wearing your red.' She herself had put on a flowing Indian cotton dress and threaded yards and yards of beads through her long fair hair.

'You told me this was a special party to mark Hamish's friend Keith getting a senior reg job. And surely he lives in that tarted-up block in the Canongate — not a tenement.'

'Yes, but it's still basically a tenement,' insisted Kirsty. 'Where are you going?' she asked as Tansy headed for the door.

'To change into my red.'

'Och, don't be daft. You look fine. Anyway, there isn't time. Hamish'll be here any minute.'

'You're quite sure that Keith'll not mind a gate-crasher?' Tansy asked doubtfully.

'Positive. He told Hamish several times that he hadn't got enough nice girls coming, and you're not going to deny you're one of those, are you?'

Tansy giggled and Kirsty said approvingly, 'That's better. Now hold on to that smile; it's a party not a wake we're going to. I wonder what's keeping Hamish?'

A honking in the street below announced his arrival, and, wrapped in their warmest coats and carrying their party shoes, the girls clumped down the stairs in boots and scuffed through the snow to the car.

'You're both looking fabulous,' Hamish told them, kissing each impartially. 'I can see I'll have my work cut out fighting off the opposition.'

It was only a ten-minute drive to the Palace end of the Royal Mile, but they spent as long again searching for a parking place. It was hopeless; the Canongate was lined with cars from end to end. 'This parking business is getting byond a joke,' muttered Hamish, getting out and unhooking the chain which guarded the entrance to the private lot behind Keith's building.

'Are you allowed to do this?' wondered Kirsty as they drove in.

'Probably not, but I'm past caring,' returned her future husband. 'But don't worry, darling. If I'm caught, I'll surely be out of gaol in time for the wedding.'

Having discarded their coats, they obeyed the notice pinned to the front door and helped themselves from the bar set up in the hall before entering Keith's enormous, low-ceilinged sitting-room. It was packed and they soon gave up the attempt to locate their host in the crush.

Within minutes, Tansy was separated from her friends, and, not long after, a surge in the crowd behind her forced her hard up against, of all people, Struan McLeod. His firm masculine outline was denting her soft flesh, something Tansy was finding both delightful and dangerous. His smiling blue eyes bore all-seeingly into hers as he purred satirically, 'Too much booze, perhaps, but I thought I was in Edinburgh—not Fife.'

'Well, so you are,' she returned, not very wittily.

'Drunk—or where I thought I was?'

Tansy went for dignity, which wasn't easy when she was practically welded to the person she wanted to impress. 'You know quite well what I meant,' she said haughtily.

'But do I?' he wondered. 'Only yesterday, I heard you say you were going to a party in Fife tonight.'

Tansy took a deep breath and spelt it out. 'I had intended going home for the weekend, but I was obliged to cancel in view of the weather. What's so extraordinary about that?'

'Nothing—if that's really how it is.'

'Why would I lie to you?' she asked unwisely.

'Now there's a question,' he purred.

And all the time, there they were, still jammed up against one another, a contact that was swiftly eroding Tansy's common sense. She made a supreme effort. 'I think you're trying to pick a quarrel,' she said loftily. 'And as this is supposed to be a happy occasion, I'm not going to oblige. Would you move, please? I've just spotted a particular friend.'

'I'll try,' he agreed, flattening himself against the wall. 'And you can tell him I'm sorry for him,' he hissed in her ear as she squeezed past with the greatest difficulty. And not only with difficulty. Her pulse-rate was climbing to an alarming level.

'Tell who?'

'That special somebody you're going on about.'

'He doesn't need your sympathy,' she hissed in return, just before being sucked back into the crowd.

Already Tansy was bitterly regretting the line she'd taken with Struan, and it didn't make sense. If there was one man in this room, in the whole world, that it would be madness to tangle with, that man was Struan McLeod. Look around, you fool. There must be *somebody* here you can talk to.

Fearful of spillage in that crush, Tansy had put her drink down minutes ago and she was wondering whether it was possible to get out to the hall and get another, when she came face to face with Morrie Gould. Her heart sank. Morrie had made numerous clumsy passes at her over the years, and the gleam in his washed-out, pale beige eyes suggested he was about to make another. Heavens, what an evening this was turning out to be! So much for Kirsty's rehabilitation programme.

'The answer to all my prayers,' wafted over her on whisky-laden breath as Morrie made his grab.

'Leave me alone,' she ordered without too much hope of being obeyed. Morrie was worse than a limpet for clinging.

'When are you going to admit that you secretly adore me?' he demanded with breathtaking audacity.

Crushed against his barrel-shaped form like this made it well-nigh impossible to say anything, but Tansy made her point by stamping hard on his foot. 'Let me go, you great oaf,' she insisted as his arms slackened.

'Yes, leave her alone, Morrie, you fool,' ordered Struan, appearing miraculously at that moment.

Tansy put out a hand and grabbed his sleeve as though it were a lifebelt. 'Oh, thank you, Struan,' she breathed gratefully. And then the sight of a luscious redhead clinging to his other arm suggested that she had warmed to him a little too late.

'I do hope I was right in assuming that Morrie is not your particular friend,' Struan returned maddeningly as Morrie retreated, vanquished. He wasn't very brave.

Tansy went scarlet with rage before hissing, 'You're absolutely impossible!' Then she dived into the crowd once more. This time her retreat was accompanied by the redhead's tinkly, derisive laughter.

When somebody called out that there was supper on the go, a lot of people surged through to the dining-room, so movement here became easier. Tansy wandered aimlessly about, speaking to this one and that and willing the evening to pass. Kirsty and Hamish were obviously having a great time, so the early escape she'd been hoping for seemed doomed. At least Morrie was nowhere to be seen now. Neither were Struan and his redhead.

Tansy wandered into the dining-room and helped herself to some food, finding herself beside a stranger who smiled at her winningly and told her his name was Clive. He was nice-looking, well-spoken and intelligent and they chatted easily for so long that Tansy allowed herself to think her luck was changing, until Clive made it clear he was prospecting for a one-night stand.

'Sorry—not my scene at all,' she told him firmly as soon as she picked up his signals. Then she left him before he could call her frigid, or Victorian, or any of the other epithets men kept for such occasions.

It was now nearly one o'clock and Kirsty and Hamish were still the life and soul of the party. At this rate they'd be staying to breakfast, so Tansy found the phone and rang for a taxi. Then she put on her coat and boots, stuffed her shoes in her pockets, and stood by the bedroom window, watching out for it. When she saw it inching its way down the steep and narrow cobbled street, she hurried down to the outside door, only to find that the taxi ticking over at the kerb had come for several other folk. Meanwhile, the door had clanged shut behind her. There would be too much noise in Keith's flat for anybody to hear if she buzzed, and it was far too late to ring any other resident and ask for re-entry. Never mind, her own taxi would be here at any moment.

Half an hour later, Tansy was still huddled in the doorway, cursing spring-doors and winter weather. The cruel east wind would have penetrated fur, and her coat wasn't even all wool. She was blue with cold and her teeth were chattering.

At the sound of laughing voices and scurrying feet on the stairs behind her, she stepped forward hopefully, but the first person out was Morrie. She shrank back in her dark corner, scarcely daring to breathe as he lurched drunkenly towards his car. Trust him to come early and grab a space. He was actually getting in when some tactless idiot called out, 'Night, Tansy.'

'Waiting for me?' called Morrie, staggering back across the slippery pavement.

'You know very well I am not,' she retorted as frostily as possible.

'Aw, c'mon,' he wheedled, grabbing her arm and yanking her bodily towards the car.

Resisting with all her might, Tansy slipped and fell in the slush. Morrie pulled her up and thrust her bodily against the car. 'I'll scream,' she threatened.

'You do that, dear. Nobody'll take any notice.' He opened the passenger door to bundle her in, just as some more home-going guests spilled out on to the pavement.

Tansy opened her mouth and managed to yell, 'Help!' just once before Morrie clapped an icy hand over her mouth.

'I wouldn't if I were you,' said Struan in a voice of steel, coming forward and seizing Morrie in a half nelson. In his unsteady drunken state, Morrie lost his footing and landed on the pavement.

Struan left him there and turned his attention to Tansy. 'You silly little fool,' he said severely. 'I suspect he's too drunk to manage anything, but all the same——'

'You can't r-really think I l-left with him,' she fumed through chattering teeth. 'I'm w-waiting for a t-taxi that hasn't c-come.'

'She sounds very cold,' observed the redhead who had, by now, reclamped herself to Struan's arm.

'You're quite right,' he agreed, leaving Tansy in no doubt as to the type of coldness he had in mind. Then he took Tansy's arm in none too gentle a grip. 'You'd better forget that taxi and come with me,' he said heavily, steering her round her assailant, still squatting on the pavement.

As the redhead was still hanging on to his other arm for dear life, Struan had to free Tansy to feel in his pocket for his car keys. He too had come early enough to park almost at Keith's door.

'I c-couldn't possibly tr-trouble you,' stammered Tansy. She had so wanted to sound dignified and only managed to sound pathetic.

'Don't be more bloody stupid than you've been already,' ordered Struan with open impatience. 'Get in!'

'You're never taking her home,' wailed the redhead,

cottoning on at last. By then, Tansy had been roughly shoved into the back of his Volkswagen.

'What do you suggest I do? Leave her here for the next randy bastard to pick up?' Struan asked wearily. 'She may not be very friendly, but I think she's had enough aggro for one night. Get in, Sophie, if you're coming. It's going to snow again any minute.'

Sophie stopped protesting and got into the front passenger seat. She started up again, though, as soon as it became clear that she was to be dropped off first. 'Here—what's this, then? I'm not being dumped,' she yelled.

'Nobody's being dumped, but if you think I'm backtracking all round Edinburgh in a blizzard you're crazy.'

'But I hoped you'd be staying,' said Sophie, swapping her harpy's tones for a seductive wheedle.

'We've not been properly introduced,' Struan answered drolly, tacitly revealing that he had only met Sophie that night.

'You surely can't prefer *her*!' roared Sophie, switching roles again with bewildering speed.

'Right now, I'm too fed up to prefer anybody,' retorted Struan. 'But I put it to you. Would it be sensible to pass your door in order to drop Tansy off first when she lives just around the corner from me? And in a storm like this?' By now, every window of the car was completely snowed up.

'And I put it to you, I thought you were a doctor— not a bleeding lawyer—but I know when I'm not wanted,' snarled Sophie, who wasn't red-haired for nothing. 'And don't bother to call me,' she added, getting out and leaving the car door wide open.

By now, Tansy was feeling both very embarrassed and rather guilty. 'I'm really sorry for messing up your evening,' she said penitently. 'Night,' she corrected in the interest of accuracy.

Struan set the windscreen wipers to fast, but they couldn't cope. He had to get out and clear the snow with broad sweeps of his arm. When he got in again he said, 'You've done nothing of the sort. Sophie is not really my type.'

'I thought she was very attractive,' returned Tansy. For some obscure reason, she was feeling more cheerful now.

'Oh, sure, her body's all right. It's her mind I'm not too sure about.'

'I didn't know men bothered about *that*.'

'Oh, very predictable. But then you don't think much of men, do you?' he challenged as he set the car going again.

'So far, I've not had much reason to,' Tansy retorted heatedly.

'Thank you. Thank you very much indeed,' Struan said slowly and deliberately.

'I'm sorry—I didn't mean you. . . Look, I'm really grateful to you. Honestly. Oh, damn!'

That was the last word either of them spoke until Struan took the car round the corner into the terrace on a nicely controlled skid. 'What's the number?' he asked tersely.

'I could walk the rest of the way.'

'When I start something, I finish it. What's your number?'

'Twenty-three. By the second street-lamp.'

When he stopped the car, Tansy leaned forward and touched him timidly on the shoulder. 'W-would you like to come up for a drink? Coffee, cocoa—a dram?'

'That's not necessary,' he said.

'I know it's not, but I wish you would. I could still be freezing to death on that doorstep, but for you.'

'Or suffering a fate worse than death,' he reminded her.

'I thought you said he was too drunk to be dangerous?'

'One can never be quite sure about that, so please don't belittle my gallant rescue.'

'You were the one who said he was too drunk, so if anybody did some belittling it was you.'

'Now who seems to be trying to pick a quarrel?' wondered Struan.

'Heavens, but you're exasperating!' cried Tansy, her natural candour heightened by Keith's excellent punch. 'All I'm trying to do is offer you some sort of hospitality in return for bringing me home. Because I'm very grateful. I really am.'

'I accept that you mean it kindly, but I couldn't trouble you at this hour.'

'Suit yourself—but thanks again anyway.' Tansy couldn't open the car door because there was some sort of obstruction outside. Then suddenly it gave and with a slight scream of surprise she plunged straight into a great snowdrift.

It wasn't very easy to get up when you were waist-deep in soft snow and your legs were buried. She was still floundering uselessly when Struan bent down and scooped her up as easily as if she were a pound of feathers. She just had time to decide how much more she appreciated being in his arms than in Morrie's before he set her down at her door. 'Oh, you are strong,' she said foolishly.

'And you're lighter than you look.'

Tansy wasn't sure how to take that. She didn't think it could be a compliment. She fished her keys out of her

for Struan McLeod. He really was so kind. Amusing too. And very attractive. Those last two were qualities he shared with his twin. Yes, in those ways, the brothers were indistinguishable. It could have been Calum kissing me just now, Tansy realised forlornly. Oh, dear, I wish I'd never been sent to Medical and met Struan. I haven't got the experience to deal with a situation like this. But then who had? There couldn't be many girls around who had been seduced by one twin and chatted up by the other.

Tansy awoke next morning to a faint smell of frying bacon. She padded across to the window and pulled back the curtains, letting in the cold grey light. Going by the state of the street below, it must have been snowing all night. Cars, shrubs and garden walls were all just rounded mounds of white.

A quick swill under the shower before pulling on trousers and a heavy jersey, and then Tansy ambled along to the kitchen, where Kirsty was preparing a massive fry-up, while Hamish set the table. 'No need to ask if you slept well, Tans,' observed Kirsty without turning round. 'Who brought you home?' she added as the Entryphone shrilled from the hall. Hamish volunteered to answer it.

'Well?' demanded Kirsty, just as Tansy had decided the diversion had side-tracked her.

'I rang for a taxi which didn't turn up and I was wondering what to do, when Struan McLeod came out with his girlfriend and offered me a lift.' Surely not even Kirsty, with her overactive imagination, could make anything of that.

'I've only met him a couple of times,' said Kirsty, 'but I think he's nice; quite different from his louse of a brother,' she added a second before Hamish came back into the kitchen, followed by the man himself.

Struan was carrying Tansy's missing shoe. 'Sophie phoned this morning in a great state about a lost earring,' he explained after greeting both girls. 'No earring came to light, but I did find this in the car. Yours, I presume, Tansy.'

'Wonderful!' she cried. 'I was afraid it was gone for good. But you shouldn't have bothered coming round. . .'

'Undeserved praise,' he returned laconically. 'Last night, the car got stuck in a drift before I reached the corner, so I had to come round anyway. Having found this, I thought I may as well drop it in.' He was looking at the preparations for brunch. 'But it looks as though I've chosen the wrong time.'

'Or the right, depending how you look at it,' observed Hamish. 'There is enough, is there not, light of my life?'

'Of course,' insisted Kirsty, who had already cracked another egg into the pan.

'Well, if you're sure; this certainly beats cornflakes,' Struan accepted, having already unzipped his anorak. 'But if I could borrow your phone first — I'd better phone that girl.'

'Help yourself,' invited Kirsty. 'You'll find it on the hall table.'

When Struan came back, the meal was ready. He'd been some time on the phone — long enough to have patched up last night's quarrel, Tansy reckoned. So what? Hadn't she already decided there was no place in her life for him? Therefore his life was no concern of hers. 'How do you like your coffee, Struan?' she asked, Kirsty having put the pot on the table in front of her.

'Black, please,' he returned with a polite sideways smile before answering a question from Hamish.

From then on, the girls were on the sidelines as the men took this chance to catch up. They had trained together and then followed different specialities.

Supposing I'd not gone home to swot that weekend before finals, Tansy thought suddenly. I'd not have met Calum and taken that dead-end job just to be near him. If I'd gone straight into hospital when I qualified, I might easily have met Struan first. But she hadn't, so why speculate? 'I'll make some more toast,' she muttered on noticing that the rack was empty. Catching up hadn't stopped the men eating a hearty meal.

Tansy was still curious about one thing, though. If identical twins were really as close as was generally supposed, why had the brothers gone separate ways? But perhaps Struan intended to return to Mull some day.

Kirsty must have been thinking along the same lines, because as soon as she could get in a word she said, 'I suppose you'll be wanting to get home to work as soon as you can, Struan—like all the other islanders I've known.'

'Not me,' he answered quietly but firmly. 'I want to stay on in hospital and get a consultancy—if I'm up to it, that is.'

Hamish hooted with laughter. 'That's rich, coming from the swot of our year, who walked off with the McLoughlin Memorial Medal for Medicine. *And* was the first to get a senior registrarship.'

'Your brother returned to Mull, though, did he not?' pursued Kirsty. 'And I'd always understood that identical twins thought alike in everything.'

'I didn't know that you knew my brother,' pounced Struan, leaving Tansy holding her breath.

'I don't; I only met him a couple of times,' said Kirsty. 'And then I heard — from somebody or other — that he'd returned to Mull.'

'I see.'

'But you don't want to follow him.' Kirsty liked answers to her questions.

'No — and, in answer to your remark about twins always thinking alike, I can only say that there are times when shared interests can be rather destructive,' he ended quietly. Though perfectly polite, he had spoken with a finality that not even Kirsty could override.

Tansy was remembering what Struan had left unsaid in that butcher's shop, when she'd asked him if his sister was a worry. Her assumption then that all was not well between the brothers had obviously been the right one. But there was now a lull in the conversation which nobody seemed disposed to fill. 'More coffee for anyone?' she asked, holding up the pot.

There were no takers, so she got up to fetch a tray and start clearing the table. That was the signal for a general move, and when Hamish and Struan went down to the street to dig out their cars Tansy and Kirsty started on the dirty dishes.

'He's nice,' said Kirsty as the door closed behind the men.

'Who?' asked Tansy, pretending that she didn't know.

'Struan, of course, you idiot. He's very different from Calum. And definitely not indifferent to you, Tans.'

'I don't know how you can think that — he hardly said a word to me all through the meal.'

'Perhaps not, but he did an awful lot of looking — as if you didn't notice.' She eyed her friend hopefully. 'I suppose you couldn't —— ?'

'Positively not,' Tansy cut in firmly. 'It'd be just too . . .weird. How would I ever know whether I liked Struan for himself, or just because he reminded me of Calum?'

'I see your point,' admitted Kirsty reluctantly. 'It's a great pity, though. I hate to see a good man going to waste.'

'He's not,' retorted Tansy, thinking of Sophie and the pretty staff nurse on Twenty. 'Going to waste, I mean. There are plenty of girls ready to take on Struan McLeod. Why do you think he's in such a hurry to dig out his car? He's probably got a heavy date lined up.'

But there Tansy was wrong. When Hamish came back some two hours later, Struan was with him.

'The cars are still stuck, then,' assumed Tansy. She was secretly pleased to see Struan, cross with herself for that, and determined not to let it show. 'You must be very disappointed, Struan. I do hope the engine hasn't seized up in the cold. I feel very responsible.' And I'm sounding absolutely ridiculous. What's the matter with me?

'Does she often rattle on like this?' asked Struan of nobody in particular. Hamish had gone into the sitting-room to light the gas fire and Kirsty was making tea in the kitchen.

'I'm only trying to show a bit of interest — sympathy,' she corrected hastily, going pink and hoping that in the dim light of the hall he'd never notice that.

'And it's very much appreciated, even though it's not necessary,' responded Struan with barely suppressed amusement.

He's reading me like a book, Tansy decided, squirming inwardly. He's too bright and sophisticated by half. 'So both cars are all right, then?' she asked.

'Yes, fine, but digging them out was thirsty work, so

when we'd finished we went round the corner for a pint.'

'On top of that huge meal? Then I hope you're both sick,' reproved Kirsty, crossing the hall with the tea-tray at that moment. 'Here were we, thinking what a terrible time you were having, and all the while you were in the pub,' she went on, glaring with mock-ferocity at Hamish, now sprawled full-length on the sofa, chuckling over some item in the *Sunday Post*.

'Yes, we realised how concerned you both were when you didn't come down to give us a hand,' Hamish answered. 'Never get married,' he advised Struan. 'Women nag the heart out of you.'

'I didn't know you were married—yet,' said Struan, sitting down on the arm of Tansy's chair and arranging his arm casually along the back of it. And don't you bother looking like that, Kirsty Faulds, signalled Tansy. This is only because we're so short of furniture.

'As good as,' Hamish was saying with a great big sigh. 'Date set, church booked, mortgage arranged; I tell you, Struan, I'm done for.'

With professional expertise, Kirsty took hold of his legs, burled him round on his backside, and sat down beside him. '*I* don't want a husband who sneaks off to the pub as much as twice a year for the odd pint,' she said, 'so just say the word, sonny, and you're off the hook.'

'Oh, I couldn't do that,' protested Hamish in a high falsetto. 'Think of my reputation. Everybody would say I'd been jilted. No, we'll just have to go through with it.' He then seized Kirsty in his arms and the two of them fell about laughing.

'Isn't love wonderful?' asked Struan, staring up at the ceiling while his hand somehow found its way on to Tansy's shoulder.

'Not invariably,' she returned quietly in a sad, flat tone that had him regarding her narrowly as she sprang up to pour the tea.

After that, the four of them idled away the rest of the afternoon and half the evening in laughter and chat, grouped around the fire in that cosy little room. When Hamish said he was starving again and asked the girls what they'd got in the fridge, Struan said he had a better idea. 'They fed us wonderfully well earlier,' he said. 'Now they deserve a treat. There's a nice little Indian place I know not a hundred miles from here. . .'

It was not even one mile away, but just around a couple of corners, and they walked there in five minutes, despite the state of the pavements.

Struan was well known in the restaurant and they were warmly welcomed, mucky boots and all. 'Is so exciting, this weather,' beamed the proprietor. 'In Bombay we are not getting this lovely snow at all.'

'I'm glad somebody likes it,' said Struan when they had been comfortably settled in a secluded corner. 'It'll be murder for you tomorrow, Hamish, getting that old heap of yours up the hill to the Southern General. So what are we all having, then?'

Curry, of course; hot, strong and the very thing for such a cold night. 'I wish I could get my rice to turn out like that,' sighed Tansy when they stepped outside again.

The clouds were gone now and a million tiny stars twinkled overhead. 'It's easy,' Struan amazed her by claiming. 'You just coat it first in oil and then boil it in twice the amount of water to rice. It turns out a treat every time.'

'I suppose that's the Indian way.'

'No, it's Delia Smith's, actually.'

'I'll try it,' she vowed, laughing merrily just before she skidded on the icy pavement.

Struan quickly steadied her, then tucked her arm through his. By now the others had dropped behind, snug in their own secret world. 'I'll show you how it's done one evening very soon,' he offered. 'And don't say, "But I couldn't possibly trouble you," because it would be no trouble at all.'

'You're so nice, Struan.'

'You're sounding surprised again,' he told her in a singsong voice.

'You don't understand. It's. . .it's. . .' But there was no way she could explain.

He thought he knew. And so he did, in part. 'I know—you told me. You don't have any reason to think well of men.'

After that there was silence for a bit until Struan asked softly, 'Did he hurt you so much, then?'

'Who? I don't know what you mean,' she protested, all confused. It had sounded as if he *knew*. But how could he?

'My dear girl, it's obvious that some man has treated you very badly; you show it in all sorts of ways. But it's wrong to let one unhappy experience sour you permanently.'

'That's very easy to say when you've not been through it,' she returned in a small voice.

'And how do you know that I haven't?'

'I find that very hard to believe!' she exclaimed.

'I wonder if that's a compliment?' he asked thoughtfully.

'Of course it is! You're so—so assured and confident.'

'Window-dressing,' he claimed. 'The fact is I too was let down, and not so long ago, but I don't mean to let it spoil the rest of my life.' They had reached the house now, but Kirsty and Hamish were only just turning the corner. 'Come out with me on Tuesday, Tansy,' he urged.

'But I'm on the rebound,' she heard herself admitting.

'So am I.'

'As long as that's understood, then.' What am I saying? I must be mad. . .

Too late. His arms were round her and his mouth was on hers, stifling thought.

'No, I'll not come up,' he was saying when the others caught up. 'I've got some reports which I must do before tomorrow. See you, then — and thanks for a super day.'

His thanks had included them all and he wouldn't change his mind, despite Kirsty's urging.

Tansy stayed silent. She was busy trying to decide if or when she would tell Kirsty that she was going out with Struan.

CHAPTER FIVE

IT SNOWED again on Monday night, right on top of the rutted, frozen mess left over from the weekend falls. The buses were off all day, so the girls had had to struggle to and from work on foot. But on Tuesday morning, Kirsty got out their skis.

'Top marks for initiative,' awarded Tansy when she saw that. 'I only hope the boss appreciates all the clutter in the changing-room.'

'If that's all that worries you, try thinking how much less she'd appreciate it if we were late again.'

'You've got a point,' said Tansy, promptly exchanging her green wellies for her ski boots.

'So what's new? Am I not always right?' grinned Kirsty over her shoulder as they clumped down the stairs.

'Oh, sure.' She'd been wrong about Tansy's worries, though. Worry number one right now was whether all this snow would snarl up the city to such a pitch that Struan would decide to cancel tonight's date.

He'd been hectically busy all day yesterday with a clinic in the morning and students to teach in the afternoon, but he'd managed to tell her in passing that he'd booked a table at the Pheasant. In spite of her misgivings about the wisdom of having anything to do with Calum's brother, Tansy had been flattered. The Pheasant was real gourmet stuff and very, very pricey; which seemed to suggest that Struan thought her rather special. Unfortunately, the Pheasant was also several miles out of the city, up in the hills, so in these conditions it would be a miracle if they got there.

But was it the prospect of not going to the Pheasant that was depressing her, or the possibility that they'd not be going out at all? Imagine being upset at missing a date with Calum's twin! I must be a masochist, decided Tansy, as she skied along in Kirsty's wake. There was no other explanation.

'I make that twelve minutes,' said Kirsty as they fetched up smartly at the back gate of the hospital and bent down to unfasten their skis. 'Perhaps we should come through the park every day.'

'We tried that, remember? It takes half an hour on foot and only ten minutes by bus. And you were the one who decided on the extra minutes in bed.'

'You can be really aggravating when you like,' growled Kirsty by way of agreement.

Not surprisingly, they were the first physios to arrive that morning, and soon afterwards, up on the ward, Sister Aitken was quite disappointed when she had to admit, 'You're very punctual today, Miss Nicholson.'

Tansy was getting her measure now. 'Just trying to follow your good example, Sister,' she returned demurely. Dr Mollie Findlay had to exit smartly before she exploded with laughter right there in the office.

Sister nodded graciously and her tone was milder than usual as she told Tansy that there were no new patients for her that morning. But she wasn't quite cured. 'So you should manage to finish on time today,' she said firmly.

'I'll certainly do my best, Sister.' You can bet your life on that. Skiing to work downhill in the grey light of a winter morning was one thing. Plodding uphill after dark, carrying your skis on your shoulder, would be quite another.

It was funny in the ward without Mrs Pringle, and the patient who'd been next to her thought so too. She jerked her head towards the drawn curtains and said in a stage whisper, 'A new one. She came in yesterday for investigations and what I don't know already about her insides would go on a pin-head. Oh, I do miss Flora.'

'Me too, but with luck you'll be away home yourself before the end of the week.' That lady wasn't for physio, but the patient on her other side was. 'So where's Mrs Allen this morning?' asked Tansy curiously.

'Away down to X-ray. Dr McLeod wasn't satisfied with her portable films.'

'Oh, dear — and so are two other of my patients. I can see this is going to be one of those days.'

Somehow, though, all the chests got done at last and then Tansy discovered that Mrs Baird had gone to Occupational Therapy and Miss Alford was having a bath. There was nothing for it but to give Mrs McIvor her strengthening exercises now.

'But you niver come to me in the forenoon,' challenged that lady.

'I know, but my schedule's all to pot this morning.'

'Ah'm no better, ye ken.'

'I wouldn't expect any improvement yet, Mrs McIvor. You've only had three treatments.'

'It would've been five, but for the weekend. Hospitals shouldna keep a five-day week. It's disgusting.'

'You could be right,' Tansy agreed peaceably, 'but that's not up to me, so let's make the most of our time now, shall we?'

'Och, you and your blether,' responded the patient, baring her wasted legs for attention at last.

The secondary anaemia which had caused her neuropathy had gone undiscovered for far too long. When

Dr Tait had asked her why on earth she'd not consulted her GP sooner, she had told him calmly, 'Och, I just thought I was getting old.' She was fifty-four.

Now she said, 'I've been having pins and needles something cruel, hen.'

'That should soon ease off now you've started the vitamin B12, Mrs McIvor.'

'And how long before I can climb fourteen flights o' stairs? The lifts are forever breaking down in our block.'

Tansy tut-tutted; another example of something she'd found out early in her training. Only fit people ever lived at ground-level. 'Now you're asking,' she temporised, 'but building up your muscle power is sure to help.' And perhaps the medical social worker would be able to help with rehousing. . .

Struan was in and out of the ward quite a lot that morning, attending to his duties with his usual mix of competence, concentration and concern. No wonder all the patients loved him. Surely somebody that committed must be equally trustworthy in other respects? But Tansy had only to remember Calum, also very good at his work, to know that wasn't necessarily so. She was at it again, trying to twist the facts to fit in with her wishes. She'd done that with Calum, and look what a disaster that had turned out to be!

'Am I getting treated now or am I not?' asked Miss Alford, by whose bed Tansy was now standing.

She came to with a start. 'Sorry! What would you say to a little walk today, once I've relaxed those stiff leg muscles of yours?'

'Make it a long one as far as the taxi rank, and you're on.'

'All in good time,' Tansy was saying with a smile

when Sister came bustling up to warn her that lunch would be served in five minutes.

'Thank you so much for reminding me,' she returned, determined not to be ruffled, since that was probably what the old so-and-so was hoping for. 'Sorry, Miss Alford, we'll have to make it this afternoon now.'

Struan was hovering in the corridor when Tansy went to get her cardigan from the cloakroom. 'Lunch?' he asked with an engaging quirk of one eyebrow.

'That's a very nice idea,' she considered, 'but today's our day for the weekly staff meeting in Physio.'

He shrugged. 'Too bad. Still, I'll come round that way with you and we can talk about tonight. Heading for the hills with the roads in their present state might be a bit silly, don't you think?'

'Yes, I do, but never mind. Another time, perhaps. This is definitely the weather for a quiet night by the fire.'

'Your place or mine?' he asked.

'I thought you were calling the whole thing off,' she said, cross with herself for being so glad that he wasn't.

'Sometimes — most of the time, in fact — I don't know what to make of you,' Struan said with a slight frown. 'Could be that's why you interest me. Now kindly listen very carefully. The Pheasant expedition is on hold until the weather improves — and what I was about to suggest when you jumped so swiftly to the wrong conclusion was that we should go instead to that new French place near the King's theatre, which as well as being excellent is also within walking distance of home. Have I made my meaning quite clear this time?'

Tansy had to smile at such perception and good humour. 'Yes, thank you, Struan — very clear indeed. Even I got the gist of that.'

'And?'

'I think it's a very good idea.'

Struan gave a sigh of mock-relief. 'Well, thank heaven for that,' he said. 'So can I take it you'll be ready when I ring your doorbell at seven?'

But Kirsty might not have gone out by then and I haven't told her yet. . . 'Could you possibly make it half-past, please? Sometimes I don't get away from here until nearly six.' Tansy was really glad that was true; she was coming to realise that she didn't want to lie to Struan.

'Seven-thirty it is, then.' His grin was ever so slightly crooked. 'Nobody could accuse you of putting pleasure before work,' he added as he left her at the door of Physiotherapy.

He knows I'm in two minds about him, realised Tansy as she hurried to join the others now crowding into the staffroom for the meeting. I wonder how he'd react if he knew why?

Mrs Dewar, the superintendent physiotherapist, always said she knew fine that none of her staff ever read the endless stream of memos put out by Admin to be pinned up by her on the noticeboard. So she had recently instituted these weekly meetings. That way, she could force-feed relevant bits of information and nobody could wail, 'But I didn't know,' when caught out on such points as parking without a permit—or failing to provide authorisation for nocturnal taxis!

Today, Tansy didn't hear above half of it, being much too occupied with the weighty problem of what to wear that night. Any of her most becoming outfits would look pretty silly with wellies, yet if she wore her good leather boots they'd never be the same, what with the snow and salt. . .

'Tansy!' Tansy blinked and looked guiltily in Mrs

Dewar's direction. 'Answer the phone, please, dear.
You're nearest.'

Tansy took the message from a patient who couldn't
attend that afternoon and resolved to keep her mind on
the present. That had been a near squeak.

'What a waste of time these meetings are,' grumbled
Kirsty as the two girls made their way to the wards
afterwards.

'Easy to say when you don't have the responsibility
for keeping us all informed,' returned Tansy. But who
am I to say that? I wasn't listening. . .

Kirsty snorted. 'You're getting quite middle-aged,
you know that? If you don't find yourself a man
soon. . . Which reminds me! My man and I are going
to look at a house in Colinton right after work. It
sounds a real bargain. He phoned me right in the
middle of the ward round, the cheeky thing! So don't
wait supper for me.'

'You're brave—with the roads in such a mess.'

'Don't forget that old heap of Hamish's is a four-
wheel-drive job. See you, then, Tans. Tomorrow most
likely.' And with a cheerful wave, Kirsty peeled off
towards Surgical.

'I still haven't told her I'm going out with Struan and
now I don't have to, thought Tansy, as she turned into
the medical block. Until next time. If there is a next
time. Do I want there to be a next time? Oh, God—
I'm so mixed up. . .

Miss Alford was frowning over a crossword puzzle
and greeted Tansy with relief. 'Never mind my
wretched leg,' she said. 'Give me something to increase
the bloodflow to my brain. I can't get started on this
ruddy thing today.'

'Sorry, that's outside my remit,' laughed Tansy. 'It
says on your referral card as plain as anything—"meas-

ures to reduce spasticity and increase function of the right leg".'

'Gobbledegook,' considered the patient.

'Maybe — but the doctors do like to pretend they know something about physio.'

'Thanks very much,' said Struan who just happened to be passing. 'I wrote that card and, as it happens, I do know something about it. My mother is a physio.'

'You never told me that!' exclaimed Tansy.

'I was saving it,' he grinned before striding on to whisk the curtains round a patient further down the ward and disappear behind them.

'He likes you, you lucky girl,' said Miss Alford, sounding quite envious.

'That's nice,' returned Tansy absently. Struan hadn't told her about his mother — fair enough. But neither had Calum. He'd been so tight-lipped about his family and every other detail of his life that anybody less besotted than she would have wondered about that long before she had.

'I was like you once,' said the patient. Tansy turned surprised brown eyes her way. 'Taking admiration as my right, just because I was pretty. Oh, yes, I was,' she repeated as though Tansy might not believe her. 'But I kept it up too long. When I did feel like settling down, I discovered that all the best bargains had been snapped up. And I'm telling you, lassie, that a dog and a good pension are no substitute for a man about the house when you can't get the top off a jar of jam and the grass needs cutting.'

By now, Tansy was scarlet. 'For heaven's sake keep your voice down,' she hissed. 'Dr McLeod will hear you.'

'Not above all the din that old besom in the next bed is making, he'll not. What are they doing to her?'

'Trying to give her a blanket bath, I think. Now, then, over on your tum, Miss Alford,' said Tansy with determination and before the oracle could give out any more advice. 'I've just remembered a really good way to retrain your dorsi-flexors — that is, the muscles that pull up your foot. I watched you walking back from the bathroom this morning and you're still tending to catch your toe.'

'I wondered when we'd be getting down to work,' retorted Miss Alford, determined as ever to have the last word.

Mrs Strang was next. If only she didn't talk so much! Neuro patients took long enough to treat as it was. She was improving, though. This time last week, she hadn't been able to hold a fork or a pencil. Thank heaven for ice and its power to lower abnormally high muscle tone. Now for some balance exercises; she's usually too nervous to rabbit on when she's standing. . . Oh, help! It's nearly four and there's still Tam Buckie to see before I start on the final round of the chest patients. . .

'Tam's away to the doctor's room for a wee crack with Dr Tait,' said the nice old gossip in the next bed. 'There's a changed lad since they stopped the auld yin coming in and tormenting him.' And also since they got Tam to face up to his unconscious, thought Tansy. She decided to do the chests now and leave Tam till last. Not that he needed much physio now that his confidence was returning.

'How do I go about suing?' demanded Tansy's newest chest case when she was tucking him up again after treatment. She blinked. He'd sounded as if he really meant that. 'I came in to the hospital to be cured, not flayed alive!'

'I did explain that percussion was necessary to shift

the phlegm that's clogging up your lungs,' returned Tansy, putting it as plainly as she could.

'And I thought you meant like when the doctor taps your chest. Your version is more like being jumped on by a cart-horse.'

Thanks very much for the compliment, thought Tansy, as she pointed out how well her tactics had worked. 'And you're less breathless too,' she added. 'That's because your airways are clear.'

'Mebbe. I'm just black and blue instead.'

Tansy was getting quite alarmed. She lifted his pyjama jacket for a quick check. 'No, you're not, Mr Downie — honestly. Not even a bit pink. And I do know how it feels. We learn by practising on one another — and our teachers. . .' She stopped because her patient was now grinning broadly.

'You're such a serious wee soul, I couldn't resist winding you up,' he said. 'Do you not know when you're being teased, lassie?'

'Not always,' she admitted. 'And you certainly had me fooled. You're an awful man, Mr Downie.'

He laughed as though she'd paid him a great compliment. 'You'll not be forgetting William Downie in a hurry, I'm thinking.'

'Not if I live to be a hundred,' she promised. 'What a fright you gave me!'

Tam Buckie was in great form. 'I'm getting home tomorrow — well, not home, actually. I'm going to stay with a pal.' There was no need for him to tell her why.

'I think that's a great idea, Tam, but you'd better come back as an out-patient. A course of graded, weight-resisted exercises ——'

'Just what Dr Tait said — he's going to discuss it with you. Will you be treating me?'

Tansy explained that she only worked on the wards.

'But you'll be well looked after down in Physio,' she
promised. 'And now I'd better dash—I'm not quite
finished yet, and I don't want Sister chasing me. Good
luck!' And she escaped before he could ask her out, as
a sixth sense warned he was about to do. She liked him,
but not in that way, and a refusal would have hurt his
pride if nothing else.

So hasty was Tansy's retreat that she cannoned into
Sister, thus earning herself a long-winded lecture on
clumsiness, haste and a deplorable eagerness to get off
duty. Considering she usually gave Tansy a blast for not
leaving soon enough, that was illogical to say the least.
'I couldn't agree with you more, but, if you'll excuse
me, I was on my way to discuss Mr Buckie's future
treatment with Dr Tait,' said Tansy, woman to woman,
when Sister eventually ran out of steam.

Yes, I'm getting your measure, you old bag, she
thought, noting Sister's pop-eyed expression with great
satisfaction. And I'll bet you'd blow a gasket if you
knew how I'll be spending my evening!

Despite the filthy streets, Tansy recklessly put on her
beautiful black leather boots with her best Laura
Ashley and her nearly new Oxfam Burberry. Surely a
girl could live dangerously now and again? She also
splashed herself liberally with the last half-inch of the
Madame Rochas which had been Calum's last present.
She wasn't quite clear whether that was because she
liked the stuff, or because she needed to remind herself
of Calum as insurance against his brother. Was there
any way at all to resolve this tangle? I should have
stuck to my original decision and kept Struan at arm's
length, she decided just as he rang the doorbell.

'You look like a million dollars,' he said when he'd
swept her slowly from head to toe with a very appreci-

ative glance. Then he leaned down and kissed her lips, which were already parted — though only to answer him. It was a heady, unsettling start to the evening, so unsettling that Tansy only remembered at the last minute to lock the door.

'So Kirsty is out, then,' assumed Struan as he followed Tansy down the stairs.

'Yes. She and Hamish are away to the south side, looking at yet another house.'

'I thought they'd decided on the one at Fairmilehead.'

'So did I, but somebody who works with Hamish told him about this one. Apparently the owner is going abroad, so it's reasonably priced for a quick sale.'

'When are they getting married?'

'On Easter Saturday.'

'Then they'll need to make up their minds soon,' said Struan as they reached the street. 'No, this way.' He grabbed her arm and turned her round. 'Longer walk, but cleaner pavements,' he explained. 'I sussed out the best route on my way here.'

'You're so considerate,' she told him warmly, because considerate was something that Calum most definitely was not.

'You're sounding surprised again,' stated Struan.

'Well, it's not a — a universal male characteristic,' she returned defensively.

'Just as not all women are so suspicious?' he asked.

'Once bitten. . .' she began.

'Only once?' he asked. 'I thought it must have been at least a dozen times. You should have more faith in yourself.'

'Or grow an extra skin.'

'I hope you're not implying that you need protection from me,' he said, contriving to sound aggrieved.

'I was speaking generally.'

'Was it anybody I might know?' wondered Struan, causing Tansy to stumble and nearly lose her footing.

'Why in the world should you think that?' she asked sharply.

He pulled her arm through his and anchored her firmly upright. 'It's a perfectly reasonable assumption to make. After all, hospital staff move in a fairly restricted circle — not surprising, considering the hours we keep — so — '

'It was somebody I knew at home,' Tansy said quickly, forgetting for the moment that wasn't quite the red herring she'd intended, when Struan would know that Calum had been working in Fife just before he'd returned to Mull.

It worked all the same. 'Well, if you will get mixed up with farmers,' Struan assumed humorously. 'Perhaps you should stick to doctors in future.'

'Morrie Gould is a doctor,' Tansy pointed out with a chuckle.

'Excepting Morrie Gould — or anybody else other than present company,' Struan stipulated firmly as they turned the corner and saw the illuminated sign of the restaurant ahead.

'I've been expecting some sort of come-back,' he said when they were seated in the cosy, softly lit interior.

'And I've been trying to think of one, but I can only come up with, "That would cramp my style," and I was afraid of sounding flirtatious. Which I'm not.'

'I'd kind of noticed that,' he returned, a little smile playing about the corner of his mouth.

'You probably think I'm a — a humourless prig,' she suggested on a slightly interrogative note.

Struan laughed then. 'Come off it! Would I have

asked you to share my precious free time if I thought that?'

'No—that's not really very likely. . .' Tansy was dying to know what he really thought of her and couldn't think how to get him to tell her.

She got a partial answer when a silent waiter brought to their table a long-necked bottle in an ice bucket, then deftly poured the pale sparkling wine. 'Champagne? I say—*what* a treat!' Suddenly she made up her mind that there was nothing to be lost by making the most of this evening. 'My spare time is limited too,' she added, smiling. 'That's why it's good to have somebody—nice to share it with.'

Struan looked astonished. 'And the cork is hardly out of the bottle,' he marvelled. 'Drink up, then, Tansy. There's plenty more where that came from. Any ideas for a toast?'

'To Kirsty and Hamish,' she said promptly.

Struan shrugged. 'All right, then—Kirsty and Hamish it is. Though I'd have said they were doing well enough,' he added afterwards.

'Good wishes never go amiss, but yes, I think they are. And I hope they always will.'

'So do I; and now let's leave them to work out their own salvation, shall we?' He topped up her glass, saying thoughtfully, 'Tansy is such a pretty name. Some sort of flower, is it not?'

'A common wild plant, formerly used as a flavouring,' she quoted.

'You would certainly add flavour to any situation,' said Struan. A shade too glibly, she thought.

'Thank you, but as Tansy is not really my name I don't feel obliged to live up to it.'

He seized on that as she might have known he would.

'So what is your name, then, you flavoursome young person?'

'Um — everybody calls me Tansy.'

'You're hedging,' he challenged.

'So would you — in my position,' Tansy answered with a little grimace.

'Surely it can't be that bad!'

'It is. My parents must have been temporarily out of their minds.'

'If you don't tell me soon, I shall die of curiosity. Then the patron will have to call the police, suspicion will fall on you and ——'

'Oh, do stop,' she implored, giggling in spite of her embarrassment. 'But you're not to tell a soul. Swear now!'

'I do solemnly swear,' he intoned slowly.

Tansy eyed him sideways. 'I'd be more likely to believe you if you weren't trying not to smile, but here goes.' She took a deep breath and revealed in a rush, 'I was named for my two grannies: Thomasina from Dundee and Alphonsine from Limoges. So I just *had* to make something of my initials — or die of teasing.' She sat back and waited for him to laugh.

'Rather than insanity, I'd diagnose far too much filial duty on the part of your parents,' said Struan firmly. 'And I think you've adapted most resourcefully.' A pause. 'But a quarter French — no wonder I sensed hidden untapped fires smouldering away there.'

When he looked at her the way he was doing now, Tansy herself was only too aware of hidden fires. She'd better go easy on the wine. Deciding to enjoy herself was one thing; getting entangled was quite another.

'Have some more champagne,' Struan was coaxing, topping up her glass before she could stop him. Fortunately the waiter arrived almost immediately, bringing them fragrant walnut soup and a basket of fresh Melba toast.

'Why do you shy away from compliments, Tansy?' Struan asked perceptively.

Because it's when you pay me compliments that you're most like Calum! 'I—didn't realise I did,' she temporised. 'Anyway, compliments aren't necessary between friends, are they?'

'That's a novel point of view,' he observed. 'I wonder why you hold it? I shall have to give that some serious thought.'

He was wearing that look again—as though he was determined to see into her very soul. Tansy felt she could crack under such scrutiny. She laid down her spoon. 'I'm such a modest wee thing,' she began by way of lightening the atmosphere. 'And I come over all shy when I'm under discussion, so how about talking of somebody else? You, for instance. All I know is that you're an islander and you were at medical school with Hamish.'

His look told her he knew exactly what she was about, even before he said, 'Well, they do say that the best defence is attack. So what do you want? A potted history or just the interesting bits, such as they are?'

'I'm sure it would all be very interesting,' she insisted.

Which of course gave him the chance to say drily, 'So the embargo on compliments is just a one-way affair, then.'

'All right—*touché*,' she conceded. 'And you don't have to tell me anything if you'd rather not. Being Scots, we can always talk about the weather.'

'Or drink our soup.' But two minutes later, he did begin to tell her things, painting a vivid picture of growing up on an island—the mountains, the moors, the pure air like wine, the rain, the long walks to school

along the shore, following his brother's lead into
scrapes — and usually being the one to get caught.

That figures, thought Tansy, from bitter experience.
But Struan went on to insist that was only because
Calum could run that little bit faster, and she warmed
to him some more, for not accusing his brother of
deliberately off-loading the blame.

Boarding-school on the mainland had come next, and
then the parting of the ways, when Calum had gone to
veterinary college and himself to medical school. 'We
saw very little of one another after that, acquiring quite
different friends. And of course I qualified first. Odd,
isn't it — that learning to treat animals should take
longer than learning to treat humans?'

'Animals can't tell you how they feel,' said Tansy.

'They can't tell you any fairy-stories either,' returned
Struan. 'Have you ever noticed how some patients
make up their minds what is wrong with them before
ever they see a doctor — and then supplement their
genuine symptoms with others they think they ought to
have, just because of things they've read about their
selected condition?'

'I can't say I have,' exclaimed Tansy, highly diverted
by this. 'But then physios rarely come into the picture
before the diagnosis is made.'

'Lucky old physios,' Struan was saying when the
waiter came to remove their soup bowls and replace
them with plates of *coq au vin*. He topped up their
glasses at the same time. Tansy hadn't realised she'd
emptied hers.

Perhaps it was all the wine that made her say, 'Of
course, being an only child I can only speculate, but I'd
have thought that having a brother — and a twin at
that. . .'

'I know exactly what you were about to say and I

wish I had a hundred pounds for every time I've heard it before,' Struan told her wryly. 'As I've already told you, as children we were inseparable and hardly needed anybody else. But we all have to find ourselves eventually, and that is — difficult, if one has a mirror-image.'

'I can see that,' she murmured, fascinated. She was remembering the day they had met in the butcher's, when he'd said something about Calum being a mixed blessing. And he'd said it as if he really meant it. Was that stuff about finding himself all that lay behind that, or was there more? How to find out? Because the greater the difference between the two brothers, the more chance there was that ——

'I'm very flattered,' said Struan, interrupting her thoughts.

'You are? That's nice, but why?'

'Because you obviously find my life story so riveting.'

'It is *very* interesting,' she stressed. 'I've often wondered how twins felt about each other. I mean, either sort of reinforced or else swamped.'

'Sometimes the one and sometimes the other,' said Struan. 'But mostly the other. Especially in adult life.'

'Sibling rivalry multiplied?' Tansy was hoping for still more enlightenment.

'That's as good a way of putting it as any,' he agreed. And by the way he said that, Tansy could tell she had learned as much as she was going to — at least for the present.

With the crème caramel, the waiter brought another bottle of champagne. Tansy's glass was empty again, but by now she'd stopped noticing. 'This is all so delicious,' she commented with a broad, contented smile.

'And possessed of near-magical properties too, it

would seem,' supplemented Struan with an indulgent smile.

Tansy wasn't sure what he meant by that, but she nodded all the same. She felt good, she was enjoying herself very much, and what the hell if he *was* Calum's brother? He was nice, he was good company, and last, but not least, he liked her. Wasn't that enough?

'I hope you don't mind, but I shall have to take your arm,' she decided as they left the restaurant some time later, after lingering and laughing over lots of coffee and *petits fours*. 'I'm feeling kind of unsteady. And what with all this ice and snow. . .'

'Feel free,' said Struan, stifling a chuckle as he tucked her arm firmly away under his. 'Is that enough support for you?'

'Oh, yes, I feel quite safe now.'

'That's a relief.' This time he didn't bother to hide his amusement.

'I'm not drunk, Struan,' Tansy insisted as they crossed the road.

'Of course you're not. It's just the heat in there, a little wine, and then coming out into the cold, on slippery pavements. . .'

'You're so understanding,' she breathed in admiration. 'No wonder you're such a good doctor.'

'I am?'

'Oh, yes. Everybody says so — even Sister Aitken.'

'Then it must be true,' murmured Struan as they turned the corner into Park Terrace.

Tansy had claimed she wasn't drunk, but her powers of observation were certainly clouded, or she'd have noticed Hamish's ancient Land Rover parked at the kerbside. But she didn't, and she urged Struan to come up for another coffee. Not that he needed any urging.

'Oh, dear,' she said when she unlocked the door and heard the giggles coming from the living-room.

'There's always the kitchen,' murmured Struan resourcefully, drawing Tansy unprotestingly in and then firmly shutting the door. Next minute he had swept her close and kissed her in a way that swiftly fanned those hidden fires. Instinct took over and she was responding eagerly when a door opened and footsteps sounded on the bare boards of the hall. They just had time to draw apart before Kirsty burst in.

A slow smile broke over her face as her glance flickered from Tansy to Struan and back, but to her credit she made no remark, just said that she supposed they'd be wanting the kettle and she'd got it in the sitting-room. 'Coffee or something stronger?' she offered, leading the way.

'Give the man a dram if he's not driving,' directed Hamish. He hadn't batted an eyelid either at the sight of Struan, though Kirsty was now smiling in a way that promised the third degree for Tansy later on.

'Did you like the house?' asked Tansy quickly, as they all gathered round the fire. She was determined to keep the conversation general.

'Didn't we just!' Kirsty promptly went into raptures, while Hamish told Struan practically that, while it was by far the nicest they'd seen, he had been a bit concerned about the drains.

Struan suggested ringing up a friend from their university days who had dropped out of medicine and become a civil engineer. Hamish said that was a brilliant idea and he would get in touch with old Bruce first thing tomorrow. 'And talking of tomorrow, it's very nearly with us and I have to be on duty even earlier than usual.' Which would be why he'd resisted the temptation to take Kirsty home with him.

The two doctors were hardly down to the half-landing before Kirsty shut the door and pursued Tansy eagerly into her room. 'So who's a little sly boots, then?' she teased.

'And who told me she'd not be coming home tonight?' countered Tansy, feeling clever.

'Which is why you thought you were safe from discovery,' retorted Kirsty. 'But why the secrecy? I thoroughly approve and so does Hamish.' She darted at Tansy to give her a quick hug. 'I'm so glad you got over that daft prejudice of yours. Struan may be Calum's twin, but he's a completely different personality.'

Tansy wanted to agree, yet still wasn't quite sure all her doubts had been overcome. But in her present hazy state she didn't know how to explain that—or even whether it mattered. 'Yes, he is nice, is he not?' she agreed. 'So thoughtful and amusing. I've had a lovely evening.'

'Where did you go?'

'Only as far as Toll Cross and the Bistro Mirabeau. It was to have been the Pheasant, but with the roads the way they are——'

Kirsty interrupted with a long whistle, her eyes wide. 'Good grief! You should add generous to your list of his virtues. I'm still waiting for Hamish to take me somewhere like that. Oh, Tans—I'm so pleased for you! He's just exactly what you were needing.'

'Do you know, I'm beginning to think you're right?' agreed Tansy with a dreamy smile.

CHAPTER SIX

'YOU'RE very quiet,' said Kirsty to Tansy at breakfast next morning.

'I'm tired,' claimed Tansy. 'After all, we were very late to bed.'

Kirsty looked as if she didn't know what to make of that. 'You sound about forty-five. At least. If you can't manage the odd late night at our age, when will you ever?'

Kirsty of course had slept like a log as she always did, whereas Tansy had lain awake into the small hours, sobering up and coming to terms with the deplorable lack of backbone she'd shown in going out with Struan. When she had slept, she had had nightmarish dreams about a composite Struan and Calum Jekyll and Hyde type, who was nice to her one minute and torturing her the next. Enough to make her quiet, she reckoned. And to prompt the question, can I ever be sure that I like Struan for himself and not because he reminds me of his brother? That was no basis for a relationship. Good grief, they could both end up scarred for life!

By now Kirsty was into her anorak and boots. 'Are you coming, or will I go for the bus without you?' she demanded from the door.

'Give me half a minute,' begged Tansy.

Sister Aitken was up to high doh that morning and her mania was affecting all the nurses, who were scurrying about like hunted rabbits.

Tansy paused in the doorway of the women's ward

and stared in amazement at all the bed-shifting that was going on. By the look of things, she'd be spending half the morning just finding her patients.

'You may well stare,' said the staff nurse, the only one brave enough to stop and explain. 'Dr White was duty registrar last night and, with the coronary care unit being full, he admitted an emergency into the empty bed Sister was keeping for a pet patient of hers, whom Dr Tait wants brought in today. All this stramash is intended to show poor old Whitey what a pest he is.'

'Is that all? I thought that somebody must have planted a bomb at the very least.'

'I wish somebody would — and no prizes for guessing where I'd like it put,' said Staff grimly. 'Coming, Sister!' And she was off again at the speed of light.

Presumably this manic game of dodgems didn't extend to the men's side, so Tansy decided to treat her male patients first today.

'Just the lassie I'm wantin' to see,' was Mr Downie's greeting.

'You've changed your tune,' she laughed.

'I'm fair clogged up this forenoon, hen, so you can bash me about as much as you like.'

'My name's not Bruno, Mr Downie.'

'Maybe not, but you pack a fair auld punch all the same.'

'Don't start that again,' she pleaded, 'or I might be tempted to really try my strength. No, just as you are for the moment. We'll clear the main airways before positioning you to drain the lower segments.'

'Do I get a productivity bonus?' wondered Mr Downie when he was finally clear.

'If you do, then we're going fifty-fifty,' insisted Tansy. 'You couldn't have managed that without my help.'

By then, Struan had reached Mr Downie's bed on his

usual quickie round which he made nearly every morning. 'It would seem I've come at the right time to listen to your chest, Mr Downie,' he decided, unwinding his stethoscope. 'Are you satisfied with progress, Miss Nicholson?' His tone was professional, but his expression was not.

Tansy had the funniest feeling that he was enquiring about personal progress too. 'I think things are going as well as possible in the circumstances, Dr McLeod,' she ventured. Why is it I can only behave sensibly in my mind and never when we come face to face? she worried.

'That's very encouraging,' said Struan before bending over the patient and systematically sounding every segment of both lungs. He took his time and when he straightened up he said, 'Yes, you're almost clear at the moment, old chap. The interesting thing will be to see how long it takes you to fill up again.' He turned to Tansy. 'How often are you treating him?'

'I was thinking of coming back again before lunch, Doctor—and then maybe twice this afternoon. . .?'

'Good thinking, and I'd like production measured and charted if that's not too much trouble.'

'Of course not. See you later, then, Mr Downie.'

'I expect you know this is all down to a lifetime of quarrying,' said Struan in a low voice as they moved away from the bed.

'I thought there had to be something more than post-flu complications.'

'Have you not read the case-notes, then?'

'I couldn't get near them. Sister guards that trolley as if it held the Crown Jewels.'

Struan frowned in a way that didn't look good for Sister Aitken some time quite soon. 'I'll speak to her,' he confirmed. 'Access to case-notes and X-rays is

essential for you. Anyway, to get back to Mr Downie.
He was nearly forty years working at the quarry face
until his silicosis forced him to quit. Of course they
wear masks now—and have machinery to do most of
the work—but when he was a lad it was all pick and
shovel stuff, and the men took for granted the chronic
bronchitis, as they thought it was.'

'Just like the mine workers.'

'Exactly. Some folk have paid a very high price for
their daily bread.'

'But things are much better now.'

'Are they?' he wondered. He seemed to be in a very
thoughtful mood this morning. 'We still don't know
what hazards may go with some of the newer technolo-
gies. Chemical processes, visual display units, atomic
energy. . .'

'Not to mention rock bands and discos,' said Tansy,
tuning in. 'Half the young people today are going to
end up deaf.'

'Quite so, Granny Thomasina,' whispered Struan
with a slight grin, but his face grew serious again as he
returned to his theme. 'There's a lot of interesting
research to be done. Meanwhile, it's our job to pick up
the pieces. Do you have any other problems, Tansy?
Apart from your difficulty in getting information?'

'Not really, thanks, Struan—though perhaps I should
hedge my bets with Sister in her present mood.'

He grinned widely at that. 'Very wise. How about
escaping across the road to Franco's at lunch time?'

'You have the nicest ideas,' agreed Tansy, forgetting
once more her early morning resolve to cool it. But
then, during that conversation it had been all too easy
to forget that this caring, compassionate man was twin
to the self-centred Calum.

'I'll see you there about half-twelve, then,' he said.

'That'll be lovely, Struan.'

On to her other chest cases. All were making progress except little Mrs Carswell. Of course her soaring temperature might not be due to her chest, but there was no doctor about to check with just now. If only Sister were more approachable! Didn't the ruddy woman realise it was her duty to keep staff informed? She'd better check Mrs C. again before lunch as well as Mr Downie. . .

Treating Mrs Strang was a doddle that day. There had been a particularly hard nut in her breakfast muesli and she'd broken her upper denture trying to crack it. Not even her formidable vocal powers could articulate properly without her front teeth, so, with a quarter of the usual debate, productivity was way up. 'Tho you think I'm weally impo — impwo — getting better, then?' she asked afterwards.

'You certainly are. The muscle tone in your leg is way down since we started the ice packs and taught you to move differently. And as for your hand function, we'll have you baking cakes soon.'

'No, you'll not! I can't abide baking,' Mrs Strang managed damply. Fortunately, Tansy had already moved aside.

Miss Alford was much too incensed by all the morning's stramash to give Tansy any advice today. 'I have never in my life seen so much disorganised and unnecessary activity as I witnessed this morning,' she pronounced before she'd even said good morning. 'That woman couldn't organise the weekly wash. She wouldn't last five minutes in the Army!'

'But you weren't — were you, Miss Alford?'

'Reached the rank of colonel and retired five years back,' was the answer. 'It was all I could do not to step in and direct operations.'

That would have put the cat among the pigeons. 'Oh, I do wish you had!' giggled Tansy.

'So does Dr White. He was egging me on, the naughty boy! But what have you got in store for me today?' asked the patient, getting back on course.

'Those obstinate dorsi-flexors of yours first. They're still reacting too sluggishly for my liking.'

'I understand that, but why do I find it so much easier to pull my foot up at the ankle when I'm lying on my face with my knee bent?'

'Because then the primitive physiological pattern of movement is broken.' How did one put something so complicated into a few simple words! Tansy wished she'd never started this. 'The primitive patterns are sort of—evolutionary. And standing up, putting the sole of the foot on the ground, reinforces extension, of which pushing the foot down is a part.' Heavens, I'm tying myself in knots here. She struggled on. 'Unfortunately, having a stroke reduces normal control and the reflexes take over. You'll just have to take my word for all this,' Tansy ended desperately.

'Oh, I do, dear. After all, you wouldn't tell me the best way to conduct a night training exercise, would you? So how'm I doing?'

'Marvellously. And I'm giving the muscles more resistance today too.'

'I'd noticed.'

'What in the world are you doing to that patient, Miss Nicholson?' demanded Mighty Mouse, having crept up unheard on her rubber soles, to startle them both. 'She can't be very comfortable in that peculiar position.'

'Don't you worry about me,' ordered the ex-colonel. 'Miss Nicholson knows exactly what she's doing and I trust her completely.'

'Hmm! Well, the lunches will be coming round very soon.'

'Oh, golly — and I haven't checked those two chests again,' breathed Tansy worriedly as the enemy retreated, vanquished.

'Off you go, then — you can finish me off this afternoon,' said Miss Alford. 'But not literally,' she called out as Tansy sped away.

Tansy reached the restaurant before Struan and slipped in to the first vacant booth. She'd just begun to wonder if he wasn't going to make it when he slid into the seat opposite. 'Sorry I'm late, honey. Sister grabbed me just as I was leaving. She wanted to complain about Peter White.'

'Honestly! That woman. . .' Words failed her.

'My sentiments exactly. Anyway, I pretended to think she was about to praise him for his skilful midnight diagnosis and I agreed that we were lucky to have such a promising chap on the team. That rather took the wind out of her sails.'

'I can imagine,' returned Tansy with a chuckle.

'How was William Downie when you went back to him?' Struan asked then.

'Productive, still, but less so than first thing. I made it fifteen mls the second time. And I've started that chart.'

Struan said fine, after which Tansy told him her worries about Mrs Carswell. He had also noticed she wasn't responding, and had changed her antibiotic. But all the time they were talking, Tansy had the feeling that there was something on his mind. She didn't discover what it was, though, until they'd lunched on cannelloni and were halfway back to base.

'I'm on call tonight,' Struan began abruptly.

'So I imagine, one off, one on being the rule. . .'

'Yes.' A pause. 'The thing is — I've got something on tomorrow night.'

'That's nice,' said Tansy neutrally, not sure what sort of response he was expecting. And he'd be on all weekend too. . .

'That's a matter of opinion,' he said heavily. After another pause, he asked her if she knew the night staff nurse on Ward Twenty.

'I've — come across her once or twice,' returned Tansy with sinking heart.

'I've known her for quite a while now. She's — a nice lass.'

'That was the impression I got.'

'Ages ago — long before I met you — she asked me to go with her to rather a formal dance. And it's tomorrow. Of course I'd much rather not go now, but I feel I can't let her down at the last minute. It's a formal do,' he repeated. 'Oh, Tansy — do you understand?'

'Of course. Anyway, I'm going out myself tomorrow as it happens,' she threw in as an extra. So don't imagine me sitting at home, wondering what you're getting up to!

'But not next Monday, I hope,' Struan said quickly, naming his next free evening.

'Sorry. Next Monday I'm on call.' And that was true.

'You could change that, though, couldn't you?'

Tansy felt a stab of irritation at his calm assumption and not only because it was the sort of reaction she'd have got from Calum. 'I could always try. There might be somebody willing to swap for a night when I'm not already booked up.'

'You're miffed about tomorrow,' he assumed.

'No, I'm not. That would be unreasonable,' she insisted, while unhappily aware that he was quite right.

She must show him how wrong he was. 'It's great to make new friends, but that's no reason to drop all the old ones. I'm not going to and I don't suppose you are. I'll see what I can do about Monday, though, if you really want me to.'

'Of course I do — you know I do!' he insisted as they arrived at the door to Physio.

Going to the changing-room to leave her coat, Tansy told herself that she was now off the hook. All she needed to do was to tell Struan that nobody was willing to exchange on-call duties next Monday and he'd probably get the message. And that *was* the best thing all round, wasn't it?

She began her afternoon with another look at Mr Downie. This time, production was minimal, but he told her it would be a different story later on. He was sure to know the pattern after all these years, so Tansy said she'd be back about four. Then she went to finish off Miss Alford, as arranged.

Miss Alford met her with a request to recommend a straightforward book on neuro-physiology. She wanted to read up on the background, the better to understand her condition. Sensing genuine interest and not morbid curiosity, Tansy promised to see what she could find.

That treatment completed, Mollie Findlay appeared with two referral cards for more new chest cases. 'Yet another post-flu pneumonia just when we thought the epidemic was over,' said Mollie. 'And a generalised chest infection superimposed on chronic bronchiectasis.'

'Bronchiectasis, eh? That's fairly rare, is it not?'

'We still see a few even in this age of antibiotics,' said Mollie, sounding like an elderly consultant. 'And this one is a classic. As a wee girl of six, she had a peanut go down the wrong way. Nobody thought too

much about it, she didn't see a doctor, and so of course
she developed a chronic lung abscess.

'And is there anything else I should know about
them, please, Mollie? Only Sister's in the office right
now, and you know what she's like if anybody so much
as glances towards the case-notes.'

'Not any more. Not after the telling-off Struan
handed out to her just before lunch,' chuckled Mollie.
'He made it plain that all staff treating patients must
have access at all times.'

'Wonderful! I'll go and put that to the test right now.'

'Only if you replace them exactly as you found them,'
growled Sister when Tansy made her request. She
squashed the impulse to say she'd had it in mind to put
them through the shredder, but couldn't resist saying
that putting them back where she found them had
always seemed the sensible thing to do.

The afternoon wore on, yet, despite being busy, it
seemed to be dragging. Tansy found herself constantly
looking round to see if Struan was in the ward. Finally
she remembered that there was a clinic that afternoon.
She had to go home without seeing him again that day.

Kirsty was on call that night, so Tansy made do with
a poached egg for her supper. What more did she need
after the excellent lunch Struan had bought her?
Struan. He'd promised to sort the problem of access to
case-notes and he'd done so without boasting about it.
Calum would have. And Calum would definitely not
have told her about the dance, so perhaps the brothers
really were as different as Kirsty had insisted.

But dared she take that chance? Was every girl this
way when she met a man who attracted her? Of course
not! But then this was a rare, possibly a unique situation. If only the physical resemblance between the
brothers was not so complete, then it would be easier

to see them as two separate people, each different, each himself. . . Oh, hell! She was going round in circles yet again.

Tansy leapt up and crossed to the bookcase to find something that would meet Miss Alford's requirements. After that, she phoned her father, did a bit of washing, and cleaned her boots. When Kirsty arrived home at ten-thirty, yawning and exhausted, Tansy was washing her hair. Towelling it dry, she went to ask how the evening had gone.

'At it practically non-stop and now I'm absolutely knackered,' returned Kirsty. 'Still, barring emergencies, I'm in for the night.'

'Would you like a coffee?' offered Tansy.

'No, thanks. I had one with Struan about half an hour back.'

'Where? There was nobody on Medical for treatment tonight.'

'We were both called to Geriatrics and you know how kind Sister Paterson is. Her kettle's constantly on the boil. We talked about you,' Kirsty added.

'I didn't realise Sister Paterson knew me that well,' mumbled Tansy from under her towel.

'Don't be coy with me, dear,' ordered Kirsty sternly. 'You know fine I meant Struan. He's really gone on you, Tans.'

'That'll be why he's taking Staff Norton to a dance tomorrow night.' Now why did I tell her that? It wasn't necessary. . .

'He's *what*?' Kirsty was thunderstruck.

'You heard. Apparently they're very old friends.'

'Are they indeed? I didn't know that. So what's his game?'

'I don't think he is playing games. This was arranged ages ago, I gather.'

'Then he should jolly well have unarranged it, if he's really interested in you. Dating two girls from the same hospital at the same time is definitely not on. You take a firm line, you hear?'

Tansy heard. It would have been difficult not to with Kirsty sounding so fierce. 'God, I'm so mad that I almost forgot to ring Hamish,' she continued. 'That civil engineering pal of his was going to look at the house for us this afternoon and I'm bursting to know what he thought of it.'

While Kirsty made her call, Tansy tried to sort out her feelings. Kirsty's unexpected indignation had rekindled the anger she'd felt when Struan had told her about his date tomorrow. He'd smoothed her down, though, with his speech about not letting Jean Norton down. Now here she was mad at him again; yet all the time Kirsty had been attacking him so vigorously, she'd wanted to defend him. It's not like that, she'd wanted to say. He only wants to spare her pride. Only I wasn't sure enough of that to stick up for him. And it's because I'm so short on confidence that I can't handle this thing. Oh, hell! Why does life have to be so damned complicated?

It was late on Friday afternoon before Tansy had any conversation with Struan — apart from the occasional exchange about patients, and then always with other staff around. Being Tansy, she ascribed this to design on his part. After all, he'd made plenty of chances to talk to her that first week, hadn't he? Busy or not, he could have talked to her today and yesterday, if he'd wanted.

So when he came bounding after her as she humped the ice canister down the corridor, as she was going off duty, she said simply, 'I suppose there's a patient I've overlooked. Who is it?'

To that he merely said in a challenging voice, 'I rang you last night.'

Tansy put down her heavy load. 'But I told you I was going out.' She'd gone with Kirsty to view the Colinton house, which had been given the all-clear. And then, because Hamish was on call, they'd bought three fish suppers and gone round to his place to keep him company.

'Yes, I know you did, but I thought I might catch you before you went.'

'I went out straight from here and didn't get home till after midnight.' What do you think of that, then? Not much, judging by that frown. Encouraged, Tansy went on, 'I'm surprised you had time to make phone calls when you had such a heavy date. How *was* the dance, by the way?'

'I didn't exactly enjoy it, if that's what you're implying,' he retorted truculently.

'I'm sorry to hear that — I had such a pleasant evening myself.' She realised with something of a jolt that they were on the verge of quarrelling. Was that good or bad?

'And I'm sorry to hear *that*,' he said heavily. 'I spent the whole damned evening wishing I'd been less bloody noble and told Jean I couldn't go. And if you'd been a bit more friendly yesterday, instead of dashing off like a hare every time our paths crossed, I probably would have!'

'But I didn't. . .' she was beginning. Yet if it had seemed that way to him. . . 'I wasn't avoiding you, but I was extra busy. Bill has been tied up with students every day this week. . . As a matter of fact, I thought you were avoiding me.'

Struan simmered down at that, staring at her thoughtfully for several long seconds before saying, 'In that case, I don't suppose you've done anything about changing your on-call, then.'

'I'm afraid not.'

'And I suppose it's rather short notice now.'

'Yes — besides, I'm fairly near the bottom of the heap when it comes to favours.'

'Would Kirsty — ?'

'Not now they've decided to make an offer for that house. Hamish will be off on Monday night and they'll have things to do.'

Struan sighed. 'So that's it, then. Unless you come round to my place for that lesson I promised you on boiling rice. Will you be in tonight?'

Tansy still wasn't sure whether or not she should go on with this. 'As far as I know,' she allowed.

'I'll give you a ring later on, then. Sorry I can't carry this brute of a thing down for you,' he added, bending down and picking up the canister, 'but I'm waiting for the boss to come and see his latest admission.'

'Bosses are such a nuisance, are they not?' asked Tansy with a tentative smile as she backed away.

'Not nearly as much of a nuisance as wee girls who can't make up their minds,' Struan retorted pointedly as Dr Tait came steaming up the corridor, white coat tails flying.

Tansy went on her way feeling much happier. He likes me — he really does — she reasoned. He must do. Otherwise he'd not be so patient with my shilly-shallying. And I like him. Yes, I do. I still wish he didn't look so much like Calum, but that's not his fault. And Kirsty is right; he is very different underneath. She had conveniently forgotten Kirsty's vehement condemnation of him when she had heard about Jean Norton and the dance.

Kirsty talked ceaselessly all the way home on the bus. Hamish's written offer for the house had been accepted in writing, so now, under Scots law, the bargain was sealed. Tonight, they were going out for a meal to celebrate, and Kirsty was over the moon. 'Only to the wine bar across the road from the Southern Hospital, as he's on call again tonight, poor darling,' Kirsty rattled on. 'It's such a relief to have found our dream house after all those months of searching. I was beginning to think we'd never. . .'

Tansy switched off. In her present state, Kirsty would be quite satisfied as long as she went on smiling and nodding. Tansy decided to be very nice to Struan when he rang her later. He'd be quite overwhelmed to find her so forthcoming. Such a pity he was on duty this coming weekend, otherwise—— She jumped when Kirsty tugged at her sleeve and said, 'Come *on*, dozy! This is our stop!'

When her friend had changed and gone out again, Tansy cooked and ate an omelette, then settled down to wait. She had to wait so long that her new-found confidence and goodwill were starting to evaporate by the time the phone rang.

'Tansy—thank heaven you're still up. Did you think I'd forgotten?'

She dodged that. 'I suppose you've had a very busy evening.'

'That's an understatement. I didn't even get supper.'

'Struan—that's awful!'

'It was well worth it, though, to hear you sounding so concerned,' he returned, sending little shivers down her spine in the time-honoured way.

'And are you still at the hospital?' she asked, keeping up the sympathy.

''Fraid so. Is that not cruel?'

Tansy giggled. 'Now you're overdoing the angst. I know you love it, really.'

'Not when it keeps me away from you.'

'I'm — thrilled.'

'Tell me something, Tansy. Would you be as encouraging face to face as you are on the other end of the phone?' Struan wondered perceptively.

Tansy was wondering that herself. 'And would you be so persistent?' she hedged.

'Try me,' he challenged.

'What — now?'

'Hardly. Mollie's just come looking for me. But tomorrow night, if things are less hectic, I could come round and give you that rice-boiling lesson.'

'That sounds harmless enough,' she decided. 'So why not?'

'Get out your biggest saucepan, then. Bye now — darling.'

She'd done it now, hadn't she? Never mind. She had things in perspective now and life was looking good again for the first time in almost a year.

Next morning, the flat got the going-over of its life, and in the afternoon Tansy went shopping for food. Then she made a beef curry, because boiled rice on its own didn't make much of a meal.

The phone rang just as she was popping it in the oven. It was Struan. 'You're not coming,' she assumed, on a surge of disappointment.

'Don't be so gloomy,' he said. 'Of course I'm coming and I rang a while back to say so. But you were stravaiging off somewhere.'

'Only to Tesco.'

'Then I forgive you — just so long as you didn't speak to any strange men.'

'I didn't. There was nothing at all strange about the dishy young man at the check-out.' I'm getting quite good at this, thought Tansy, feeling pleased with herself.

'I can see I'm going to have to keep a very close eye on you, my girl,' Struan said firmly. 'Perhaps I'd better come round right now and get started.'

'Fine. Just give me five to hide the milkman in the wardrobe.'

'Not on your life!' he threatened with a chuckle as he hung up.

It was a bit longer than that, though, and Tansy had made a pot of tea by the time Struan arrived. She'd hardly got the door shut when he took her firmly in his arms, kissing her long and hard before she had time to breathe. 'I thought you were going to keep an eye on me — not suffocate me,' she said a trifle unsteadily, as soon as she could. And that was not a bad reply, considering the way she was feeling.

'Just seizing my chance before you back off again,' he whispered, not slackening his hold.

'It's only five o'clock in the afternoon,' said Tansy.

Struan held her just far enough away for her to get the full benefit of his puzzled look. 'What's the time got to do with anything?'

'I just thought it was a bit early for this sort of thing.' She wasn't about to go from a standing start all the way to the finishing post in something like twenty-four hours. She might be feeling more confident, but she wasn't yet totally reckless.

'That depends on the sort of thing you had in mind,' he said with a hint of a grin.

'I was under the impression you were here to teach me how to boil rice,' she returned, refusing to be drawn on that.

'Now I get it. Five is cooking time.' He tightened his hold and gazed down into her eyes. 'How early do you consider appropriate for — the other?'

You're an awful man,' she accused softly.

'And I thought you were beginning to like me!'

'Do stop clowning and come and have a cup of tea,' she laughed, wriggling out of his arms.

'Is this your usual response?' asked Struan, following her into the sitting-room.

'That depends,' she temporised.

'On what?'

'Why, the time of day, of course,' she smiled, sitting down on the sofa.

He promptly sat down beside her and so the tone of the evening was set — laughing extravagantly at each other's jokes, cooking the rice, of course — and he really was good at that — supper, and Struan praising her half of it, then snuggling up afterwards on the sofa again. Tansy was wondering how much further down the road they would get that night — and whether she would cope — when the phone rang. 'I'll go — it could be Kirsty,' she said quickly when Struan half rose.

'Tansy? Sorry, love, but it's Mollie. If I could just have a quick word with Struan. . .'

'Sure, hold on a minute, Mollie. I'll call him.'

She returned to the sitting-room and left them to it. She had quite overlooked the fact that Struan would have to leave her number at the hospital. Of course Mollie knew or suspected, but supposing it had been somebody else calling? Jean Norton, for example. Tansy was pretty sure that by now Struan would have told her he couldn't see her any more, but had he told her why?

He came silently back into the room and crept up behind her, putting his arms around her waist and laying his cheek on the top of her head. 'Sorry, love, but I'll have to go in. Mollie's rather worried about a patient on Nineteen. I've never seen her, and it's too difficult to advise her over the phone.'

Tansy could think of some who would, but Struan wasn't that sort of doctor. 'Havers! I know it's only because you want to get out of washing the dishes,' she teased.

His arms tightened round her before he let her go, turning her gently round. 'How dare you?' he said with playful ferocity, before dropping a kiss on the tip of her nose. 'I was just about to suggest leaving them until tomorrow.'

'So you're coming back tomorrow, are you?'

'I'll come back tonight — if you ask me nicely,' he said experimentally.

'Thank you, but tomorrow will do just fine,' said Tansy.

'I'm glad you think so,' he whispered before kissing her goodbye in a way that had her just about barring his way to the door.

It was only after he'd gone that she realised there were two ways of taking his parting remark. Had he meant he was glad she wanted him to come round tomorrow, or was he glad she'd declined his offer to come back later on tonight? Tansy thought she preferred the second possibility. That would mean he'd taken the point that she wasn't a girl who tumbled into bed the minute a relationship got started — and that he was glad she wasn't.

CHAPTER SEVEN

ON MONDAY morning it was snowing again, large, damp flakes that melted as soon as they touched down. 'Ruddy weather,' growled Kirsty as she swept the breakfast things into the sink to be dealt with after work.

Tansy couldn't have cared less about the weather as she wandered along to the bathroom to clean her teeth. Struan had been on call again yesterday, but he had still managed a couple of hours with her in the evening, time he'd put to the greatest use. He was tender, perceptive and exciting—and if he hadn't entirely demolished her doubts, he had certainly caused a remarkable shift in her point of view. Struan was Struan, as different from his deceitful, fickle brother as a brother could be.

She had to work tonight and Struan was on call again tomorrow, so it would be Wednesday now before they could be together free from the constant threat of the telephone. How would it be? What would happen? The accord and attraction between them was now so strong that Tansy could guess, and she was thrilled.

Not so Kirsty. Having long urged her friend to get out there and back into the mainstream of life, she was now counselling caution. 'Put on the brakes, Tans. Take time until you're one hundred per cent sure of him,' she had advised after Struan and Hamish had left the night before. 'You can't afford to make another mistake.'

'You're saying all this because he's Calum's brother,' assumed Tansy.

'How can you say that when I'm the one who keeps pointing out how different they are? No—I think this is the real thing, Tans, so don't blow it. Whatever they say, a lot of men still appreciate a little hesitancy on the part of the girl of their choice. I've got Hamish's word for that—and I don't think that's only because he's a son of the manse. Did you know we never slept together until our engagement was announced?'

Tansy had suspected as much, but then Kirsty had always been good at timing her moves. Unlike me, she thought. I slept with Calum because he threatened to finish with me if I didn't. Yet he still walked out—and I learned the hard way that sleeping with a man is no guarantee against desertion. I ended up feeling used and diminished. Yes, Kirsty's right when she says one should be absolutely sure. The big question is, can I trust myself to know? I trust Struan, though. At least, I think I do. . .

'However long does it take you to get ready?' cried Kirsty. 'We've got exactly three minutes to get to the bus-stop!'

'Tansy—hey, Tansy,' called the senior physiotherapist on Geriatrics when the girls pelted into the changing-room with only seconds to spare.

Tansy checked in the doorway and looked back. 'Yes, Mavis?'

'I hate asking at the last minute like this, but could you possibly swap on call? I'm down to do Tuesday and now something's come up.'

'You mean—you want to do tonight?' Tansy couldn't believe her luck.

'That's right, if you can manage tomorrow.'

'No problem.' Not when Struan would be on call too. 'That actually suits me quite well.'

'What an obliging little soul you are,' said Mavis graciously. 'Don't forget to change the list, or the boss will go spare.'

Tansy would have liked to tell her to do that herself, as she was the one who wanted the change, but that would be rather short-sighted, when she'd probably be sent to Geriatrics when she'd finished on Medical. But it took time she hadn't got to amend the department list and then tell the switchboard. Tansy panted up to Eighteen five minutes late that morning.

Sister Aitken had just opened her mouth to make the most of that when her phone rang, letting Tansy off the hook for the moment.

Mr Downie was better today. His sputum production was as copious as ever, but he told her he was better, so Tansy took his word for that. With all his experience, who better to know?

The others were all improving too. Was that normal progress, or had the weekend physio been more effective than she? How much Tansy regretted spending her first post-grad year in private practice, instead of in hospital. But wait, though. If she'd timed things differently, her path might not have crossed with Struan's. You couldn't have everything. Was it really barely a month since she'd thought their meeting a tragedy?

'Tansy!' Bill Cox was calling her now. 'I'm afraid I've been neglecting you, but those students were hopeless. I couldn't let them out of my sight for an instant. Anyway, I'm free now, so if there's any help you're needing, just say the word.'

'I don't think so, thanks, Bill. My patients all seem to be improving. And the doctors are very helpful.'

'So I was hearing.' Bill gave her a broad wink. 'Well you know where to find me in case of need.'

Mrs Chisholm and Mrs Strachan, Tansy's two newest stroke patients, were both progressing well. Too well for Sister's liking. She didn't hold with all these gymnastics so soon. 'Just remember that I shall hold you responsible if there are any adverse consequences, Miss Nicholson,' she warned. And right in front of the patients too! Wonderful psychologist you are, thought Tansy.

'I am acting in accordance with Dr Tait's expressed wishes, Sister,' Tansy told her firmly, to which Sister muttered something about checking up before she squeaked indignantly away.

'She'll be the next to have a stroke if she doesn't control her temper,' Mrs Strachan observed sagely. 'Take no notice, love. You're doing a grand job. I thought my hiking days were over until you got going on my leg.'

'Poor Sister,' put in Mrs Chisholm, who prided herself on her knowledge of human nature. 'Her trouble is that she just can't abide young folk. Wasted her own youth, no doubt, and can't stand seeing others make a better job of it. I'll just pop my hand into Senga's ice bath now she's done with it. That'll save you making another, love.'

'That's a kind thought, Mrs Chisholm, but I don't think it'll be cold enough now to do the job properly.'

'The temperature of the ice bath must be low enough to depress the reflex arc, thus reducing spasticity and allowing voluntary movement,' intoned ex-Colonel Alford, who was deep in the book Tansy had lent her.

'Listen to her,' marvelled Mrs Chisholm. 'No wonder she's so good at the crosswords.'

Struan had a follow-up clinic that morning, so it was

almost lunchtime before he came to the ward. When she saw him go into the doctors' room, Tansy hurried along to tell him the good news.

There was nobody else there and he hugged her when she told him.

'You're pleased,' she observed unnecessarily.

'Of course I'm pleased, you funny wee thing. Did I not suggest you tried to swap?'

'Yes, but when I couldn't I thought you might arrange to do something else tonight.'

'Supposing I did? It wasn't something I wouldn't gladly cancel to spend the time with you. What would you like to do tonight?'

'I don't mind, Struan. Anything.'

'Anything?' he queried provocatively. 'Supposing I suggested something criminal — or naughty?'

She giggled. 'Then I should appeal to your sense of honour.'

'How do you know I've got such a thing?'

'Just hoping. I'm an optimist.'

'What a wonderful effect I'm having on you! It's not long since you didn't trust a man any further than you could push him with a feather,' he was saying when the door was flung open and in walked Sister.

'What is going on here?' she demanded harshly as Tansy took a gigantic leap backwards.

'Nothing that need concern you, Sister,' said Struan calmly. 'And as you didn't bother to knock, I shall dispense with that courtesy when next I call on you in your office. Now presumably you have a query. . .?'

'I — um — I don't like the look of Mrs Carswell.'

'That's probably mutual,' he murmured over his shoulder to Tansy, before saying to Sister, 'Then I'd better come and see how she looks to me.'

From the doorway he turned and hissed to Tansy, 'I'll pick you up at half-six, darling.'

I wonder where we're going, she asked herself as she hurried down to Physio for lunch. And I wonder what it is he's putting off so that we can? Now there was a question.

'We're only going out to the house to do a spot of measuring tonight, so you can have all the hot water for a bath if you like,' offered Kirsty as the two girls climbed the stairs to their flat that evening.

'Thanks, I think I will. One of my patients was sick over me this afternoon.'

'That's as good a reason for a bath as any I ever heard,' agreed Kirsty as she unlocked the door. 'Where are you going?'

'I don't know. And that's awkward, because I don't know what to wear.'

'Put on your Liberty skirt and that lovely deep rose sweater with the beadwork that you paid far too much for. That should cover most possibilities.'

'You're right. What would I do without you, Kirsty?'

'You'll find out, once I'm married,' said Kirsty cheerfully. 'Now away and have that bath.'

Tansy was ready too soon and spent the time sighing over her hair and tweaking the sitting-room curtains back to peer down into the street for a first glimpse of Struan's car. 'Anybody would think this was your first date ever. Show a bit of sophistication for heaven's sake,' urged Kirsty. 'No, you stay there. I'll go,' she ordered when they heard the doorbell.

Tansy heard murmured voices, a muffled laugh and then the sound of the kitchen door closing before Struan came into the sitting-room alone.

He crossed the room to kiss Tansy, before holding

her at arm's length to view her with approval. 'You look wonderful. I like you in pink.'

'I'll make a note of that,' said Tansy, who had been doing a spot of admiring herself. Calum's idea of clothes for an evening out ranged from the casual to the downright scruffy, but Struan's well-cut suits always looked as if they'd just come back from the cleaners. Tonight he was wearing charcoal-grey with a finely striped pale blue shirt and his university tie. If he ever wore jeans, they'd have a designer label, she thought. 'Where are we going?' she asked.

'To the Lyceum, if that meets with madam's approval.'

'Oh, you darling! I missed that play the first time around.'

'I know. I heard you say so last night.'

How thoughtful he is. I'm so lucky. . .

'There's just one wee problem, however. It starts at seven-fifteen, so there's no time for a meal first. Can you wait until afterwards?'

'Oh, yes — thank you, Struan. I'm not a bit hungry.' Haven't been for days. I really must be in love. . .

'But you will be by ten,' he predicted as he picked up her coat from the sofa and held it out for her to slip into.

'How did you know that was mine?' she asked. She'd worn her raincoat last Tuesday.

'You were wearing it the night of Keith's party,' he returned.

'Please don't remind me of that awful night,' she begged.

'"Awful" is too strong a word, although it certainly didn't turn out quite the way I'd hoped. Still, the next day made up for it. Ready?'

'As I'll ever be,' she said, and she didn't just mean for the theatre.

It wasn't long, though, before that confidence was put to the test. It was snowing damply again, so Struan left Tansy outside the theatre and went alone to park the car. And as bad luck would have it, the first person Tansy laid eyes on was a farmer's wife from Fife who knew all about Calum and his defection.

Too late Tansy pulled the shawl collar of her coat up over her head and moved away. 'Tansy—Tanzee!' Flora Cunningham came stumping eagerly up the steps and seized Tansy's arm in an arresting grip. 'Long time, no see. How *are* you, dear? I must say you look all right,' she added as if that were cause for disappointment.

'I'm fine, Flora, just fine.' I'm not asking her how she is; she always goes on so. . .

But Flora told her anyway.

I must get away before Struan comes or heaven only knows what she'll think or say. . .'Are you going in here, then?' she asked desperately, cutting across the saga of Flora's latest varicosed vein.

'To the theatre? Of course. I'm waiting for my sister. What about you?'

'I'm waiting for a friend.'

'How funny.' Why funny? 'We're in the upper circle. I wonder if you're anywhere near us?'

God, I hope not! 'I don't know. My friend has our tickets.'

Frantically, Tansy scanned the crowd on the pavement, dreading to see Struan's close-cropped curly dark head.

Flora was now hopping awkwardly from one foot to the other. 'You know my sister, do you not, Tansy? So if you see her, will you tell her I've gone to the ladies and will meet her inside? This cold weather plays havoc with my inside since my — prolapse.' She mouthed the last word delicately before speaking up again, promising to look out for Tansy at the interval.

She was barely out of sight before Struan came bounding up the steps and took Tansy's arm. He eyed her from under eyebrows pitched at different levels. 'What's wrong, dear? You look as though you'd seen a ghost.'

She forced herself to smile. 'Nothing so gruesome; just a neighbour who thinks that because I'm a physio I love hearing about her various defects.' Pitched just right, she thought.

Especially as Struan assumed she meant an Edinburgh neighbour. 'That reminds me,' he said. 'Mollie had a postcard yesterday from Gerda Malpas's mother, saying that the boys are settling down surprisingly well. She thought we'd like to know.'

'How very thoughtful when she must be so busy. And talking of patients, I got a buzz from Mrs Baird this afternoon. She's finding life much easier without her mother-in-law. She's very grateful to you for sorting out that problem.'

Struan was guiding her towards the stairs up to the grand circle. Tansy hoped they were placed well back, so there'd be no possibility of Flora looking down and spotting them. 'We could probably talk patients all evening,' said Struan, 'but I don't think that's a very good idea, do you?'

'There has to be something more — more. . .'

'Personal? I agree.'

'Row G,' said the usherette. 'Twenty and twenty-one — that's nearly in the middle.'

As well as far enough back for safety. Tansy breathed

more easily. 'I'm looking forward to this so much,' she said as they found their seats.

Struan agreed, but he was looking at Tansy, not the stage.

It was a marvellous performance — a believable plot, crisp and witty dialogue, and the acting was splendid. 'And everything about it Scottish,' Struan said loudly when the applause finally died away.

'I didn't know you were a Nationalist,' teased Tansy.

'Only when some Sassenach like that Hooray Henry behind us sounds so surprised that anything up here in the frozen North compares favourably with London productions. Are you hungry, sweetie?'

'I'm afraid I am — in spite of those gorgeous chocolates.' He had given her a box of Thorntons' Specials and they'd polished off the top layer.

'Could that be why you're wearing such a hunted look?' Struan asked curiously.

In fact, Tansy was preparing for evasive action should Flora loom again. 'Somebody just stepped on my foot,' she improvised.

'I'm surprised you felt it through those things,' he said. She was wearing her boots again.

'They may look solid, but the leather is quite fine.' She was loathing lying to him, but this was nothing to what lay ahead if they ran into Flora. Flora would assume that Struan was Calum, then Struan would realise that she and Calum. . . That was just too awful to contemplate! Why had she never considered before how much he would hate the idea that she had had an affair with his twin? Because until now she'd only seen this thing from her own selfish viewpoint.

'I think you must be hypoglycaemic,' said Struan anxiously when they reached the street.

Tansy turned a puzzled gaze on him. 'Why do you think that?'

'Because you're looking quite faint. And what else could cause that but waiting too long for your supper?'

'I—I hate crowds. Like on those stairs. Supposing somebody slipped? There'd be such an avalanche of falling bodies. . .' Now he'll be thinking I'm a wimp. Is that better than having him find out I'm a liar?

Struan squeezed her arm against his side. 'Poor little Tansy! I never thought of that. Never mind, love, you'll soon come to out in the open.' A quick glance to right and left and they were crossing the road. 'It's only two minutes to that nice little Italian place in Grindlay Street and the service is always prompt.'

So he had taken her stumbling excuses at face value, they hadn't seen Flora, and the situation was saved. For now. But the show-down was only postponed. Oh, heavens! How am I going to tell him?

'How about a drink to settle your jangled nerves while they're bringing the tortellini?' asked Struan when they were seated and the order had been given.

'You're the kindest man I ever knew, but my nerves are just fine now,' Tansy insisted. 'Oh, Struan, please don't see me as a poor, neurotic thing. . .' Because even though she knew now that the future wasn't nearly as rosy as she'd begun to hope, it still mattered terribly that he should think as well of her as possible.

'Darling!' He reached out across the table and covered her clenched fist in a warm, strong grip. 'Nobody who's seen you squaring up to Sister Agatha could possibly think that.'

She was instantly diverted. 'Struan! Her name isn't really Agatha, is it?'

'Not just Agatha, but Agatha Agnes.'

'That's cruel! And probably explains a lot. She should have invented something, as I did.'

There's not a lot you can make of three As — except a cry of pain,' he pointed out. 'You had better material to work with.'

'How true. Oh, poor Sister Aitken. I'll try to be much nicer to her in future.'

'Always supposing she'll let you,' he said as large plates of pasta and a wonderful salad were brought to their table.

After supper, they agreed that they would go to the Pheasant on Wednesday, unless the weather went haywire again. 'So with that settled, we can start planning the weekend,' said Struan as they left the restaurant. 'Only two minutes to the car,' he added. 'I was lucky tonight.'

But I wasn't, Tansy thought sadly. 'About the weekend, Struan. I'm afraid I'll have to go home.' And tell my side of the story before Flora does! I didn't see her again, but that's not to say she didn't see us!

'That's all right. I'll drive you.'

Oh, help! 'I'm not sure that's a terribly good idea,' she said hesitantly. 'You see, my father's not very well just now; that's why I'm going.' Partly true.

'What's the matter with him?' Struan asked inevitably.

'I don't know because he refuses to see the doctor. He gets tired very easily and has lost some weight.'

'All the more reason for me to come with you, then. I might be able to form an opinion.' They had now reached the car. Struan unlocked it and handed her in.

Now very miserable, Tansy sat there waiting for him to join her. She couldn't think how to handle this. Whatever happened, Struan and her father must not

meet until she had explained to both of them.
Separately.

'We'll make it Sunday,' Struan decided, settling
things, as he thought. 'And on Friday night, we'll go to
the concert in the Usher Hall. You shall choose what
we do on Saturday.'

'Thank you,' said Tansy as they drove off.

When they got home, the flat was in darkness.
'Good,' said Struan.

'Kirsty'll not be long.' But then again, she may not
come home at all. . .

'But she's not here yet,' he said. He tossed his coat
on to the nearest chair, unbuttoned hers and peeled it
off. Then he pulled her close to him. There was an
urgency in his kisses tonight and a hardness in his body
that was quickening her senses to fever pitch. It would
be so easy to yield, to drown all doubts and fears in
shared bliss. . .but that would solve nothing, would
only complicate things even more. . .

'Which is your room?' he breathed even as footsteps
echoed on the worn stone stairs.

'No. Oh, Struan, it's — too soon. . .'

'Or too late,' he groaned as Kirsty's key scraped in
the lock.

'Hamish is developing the most fearsome cold,' she
explained as she came in. 'I've put him to bed with
aspirin and a hot toddy, but, not being anxious to catch
it, I decided to come home.' She tuned in to the tension
in the little hall, darted an enquiring glance at Tansy,
and picked up her confusion. 'I'm going to make myself
a mug of cocoa,' she decided. 'Can I make some for
you?'

'Not for me — I'll be going soon,' said Struan. He had
himself well in hand now. When Kirsty went to the
kitchen, leaving the door ajar, he laid straight arms

across Tansy's shoulders and clasped his hands behind her head. 'You're right,' he said gently. 'It is too soon. What a good thing one of us has a bit of commonsense. But I want you, Tansy — very, very much. You do know that?'

'Yes,' she whispered. 'And I'll — not forget, only. . .'

'I know, darling. You told me.' He kissed her gently and seemed pleased with the response he got. 'You're not like most girls,' he told her humbly. 'You're special. Very special. And don't you forget it. Goodnight, my dear one.' He kissed her once more with a tenderness that brought tears to her eyes.

Then he was gone, leaving Tansy a tangle of emotions. So he thought her special — very special. But would he still think so when he found out that his brother had been there before him?

CHAPTER EIGHT

BOTH Tansy and Kirsty slept in next morning, in Tansy's case because she'd lain awake half the night worrying. Scrambling to shower and dress, running for the bus and then having to stand all the way to the hospital provided no chance for conversation, but as they pelted down the main corridor as fast as they could without actually running Kirsty managed to puff, 'You're doing well, Tans.'

'Think so?' Tansy puffed back.

'Yes. Keep it up.'

'Thanks.' But then Kirsty was still looking at things from Tansy's point of view. And Tansy had never admitted just how far things had gone between her and Calum. I should have told Struan the whole story right at the beginning, she realised with hindsight. How could she have been so stupid as not to see that?

At least Sister was away at a meeting this morning, so there was no scolding when Tansy arrived late on the ward again. She longed yet dreaded to see Struan, but he was attending to an emergency on Ward Twenty.

Tansy strove to concentrate on her work. 'Yes, it's marvellous that you're getting home, Miss Alford. No, don't worry about the book if you've not finished it. Just drop it in when you come back to clinic.

'No, I'm sorry, I've no idea when you'll be getting home, Mrs Chisholm. There's still a lot of work to be done on that hand of yours, and the doctors will be wanting to get your warfarin dosage right too. That's crucial.'

Mrs Carswell seemed better today. Had Sister's panic in the doctors' room yesterday been a false alarm, then? Tansy asked Mollie.

Mollie hadn't heard. 'But if you and Struan were having a tête-à-tête, the chances are that any old excuse would have done to break that up,' Mollie said shrewdly. 'Did you know that Staff Nurse Norton on Twenty is her niece?'

'No, I did not!' exclaimed Tansy.

'I didn't think you did. Unfortunate, is it not?' Mollie didn't need to say why. Both of them realised that Sister Aitken had probably earmarked Struan for her niece.

'I'll say! Struan might have warned me.'

'Perhaps he doesn't know.'

'That's possible.' All the same, Tansy didn't see how he could be ignorant of that.

'Or else he thought that knowing would make you nervous,' suggested Mollie.

'Nothing could possibly make me more nervous of Mighty Mouse than I am already,' said Tansy with feeling. 'Now I'd better dash. Mr Downie is more productive than ever today, so I've got to fit in another postural drainage session before lunch.'

'Rather you than me,' said Mollie, wrinkling her nose.

'I don't know where it's all coming from,' marvelled Tansy when the extra treatment was finished.

'Dr White wondered if I was starting with a fresh infection.'

'Oh, no—not when I thought we'd. . .' She peered into his sputum carton. 'Right enough, this does look a bit green. What a good thing I sent off a sample to the lab earlier.'

'We do have some lovely conversations, I must say,'

said the patient wryly. 'I feel better for getting rid of that, though, love. I just can't seem to dredge it up from the bottom of my lungs without you giving me a well-directed thump at the right moment.'

'That's what it's all about, Mr Downie. I'll be back to check you over again in an hour or two.'

'Thanks, Miss Nicholson. You're a very special wee lassie.'

'So I've been told,' she said with a laugh, but she wasn't laughing inside. How am I ever going to tell Struan about Calum? she agonised yet again as she dashed off to assess her newest patient.

Mrs Mitchell had rheumatoid arthritis. 'She's gone to X-ray,' said a very junior student nurse who was remaking Mrs Mitchell's bed during her absence. 'Surely she's not for physio? She's in far too much pain.'

Tansy blinked at such confidence. 'I have to assess her muscle power and measure the range of movement in all her joints as part of the overall picture they're putting together,' she explained.

'You can forget that. Dr Findlay did that earlier. I watched her.'

'That would only have been in a general way as part of the admission procedure,' Tansy explained patiently. 'Precise calculations of that sort are my job.'

'Duplicated effort is a waste of time and money,' said this surprising young person. 'I shall put that in my thesis.'

Cheeky wee besom, thought Tansy, wasting no more time on her. But on this ward, under Mighty Mouse, she'll soon learn.

Tansy and Struan met at last at the end of the morning, when he was coming into the ward and she was leaving it to go to lunch. Her reaction, despite her worries, was one of pure happiness. 'Oh, Struan,' she said foolishly.

Unless his eyes were lying, he felt the same. What a wealth of feeling went into a simple, 'Hello there.'

'You've had a very busy morning,' she assumed.

He grinned his lop-sided grin. 'You can say that again. And it's not over yet. How are things with you?'

'Pretty much as usual. Not having Miss Alford to treat will make a difference, though.'

'Don't bank on it—there's bound to be another to take her place. I wish I could suggest going across the road for lunch, but. . .'

'I know,' she said. 'But there's always the chance we'll run into one another when we're toiling away tonight.'

'I'm counting on it,' he said.

'Me too,' she returned, hurrying away when she noticed Sister approaching. 'Good morning, Sister.'

'Good afternoon, Miss Nicholson,' corrected Sister as she puffed past.

'Are any of your patients needing treatment tonight?' Bill Cox asked Tansy about half-past four.

'Only Mr Downie; how about the rest of the unit? I've changed on call with Mavis, you know.'

'Bad luck, lassie. There are only two cases on Twenty, barring emergencies, but wait till you see the rest of the list. ICU is going like a fair and there were three ops on the Cardio-Thoracic Unit yesterday.'

'Any by-passes?'

'Just the one, but then how many would you expect? Or do you not know how long they take?'

'Of course I do! Seven hours minimum.'

'All right, keep your nice little chestnut thatch on.' Bill looked thoughtful. 'At the next staff meeting the

ICU senior and myself are going to raise the possibility of having two physios on every evening from now on. Treatment figures are nearly double what they were this time last year.'

'The girls and boys will be very grateful, Bill.'

'That'll be a great comfort when the powers that be turn us down,' he returned ruefully. 'Well, I hope you get home this side of midnight, lassie, but don't bank on it.'

'I won't,' agreed Tansy with a sigh, and when she saw the list up there on the staffroom noticeboard she realised that Bill hadn't been joking. Struan had said he'd be looking out for her, but she doubted she'd be still long enough to be spotted.

At half-past ten, Tansy dragged herself wearily up the stairs to Ward Twenty. She wondered as she went what perverse administrator had ordained that the medical ward attracting the worst chest cases should be on the top floor. She intended to treat one of Bill's two cases a second time, because the poor lady was weak but full of secretions, and very grateful for help with coughing.

To be on the right side, Tansy had put out a call for Struan to get his backing, but the switchboard operator had told her he wasn't answering, so he must have gone home. 'Will I ring him for you?' she had asked helpfully.

Tansy had said not to bother, it wasn't that vital; she could always check with the duty house officer instead. Predictably he had said to play it safe, so here was Tansy plodding up all these stairs again. 'Is Staff Norton about?' she asked the nurse who was keeping watch in the main ward.

'She's in the office.' A pause and a disdainful sniff. 'Entertaining. Can I help?'

'I was only wanting an update on Mrs Morton.'

'She's much the same — still restless, productive and unable to cough. She'll be glad to see you, I'm thinking.'

The poor lady was too weak for vigorous coughing, but getting her to lie on alternate sides and applying gentle pressure to the chest wall at the critical moment worked wonders. 'Thank you — dear,' murmured the patient breathlessly. 'I think — I might — get some sleep now.'

'I'm so glad,' murmured Tansy, 'but I'll be here all night, so just ask Nurse to give me a buzz if you need me again.'

Tansy now had two whole hours free before she needed to visit Intensive Care again and she was looking forward to relaxing down in Physio. The office door was still shut, but a girlish giggle from behind it suggested that Jean Norton was still entertaining.

Then she heard a man's voice which stopped her in her tracks, her heart beating wildly. She hadn't made out what he said, but when Struan laughed it was all she could do not to fling open the door and confront them.

Common sense prevailed, and she was glad when the lift doors opened and two porters wheeled a recumbent figure on a trolley towards her. Struan's presence was explained. He had of course been called in again to see this emergency admission.

Down in Physio, she lay on the bed, stretching her weary limbs. Yes, Struan had the best of reasons for being up on Ward Twenty, but did he have to be there laughing with Jean Norton behind a closed door? Be fair, she told herself next minute. Were you not laughing yourself with that nice duty house officer earlier this evening? Where's the difference?

* * *

'You look terrible,' said Kirsty when she came into the changing-room next morning, as Tansy was coming out of the shower.

'So would you if you'd been in and out of ICU every two hours all night long,' yawned Tansy.

It's just wicked the way you always seem to get the heavy nights!' exclaimed Kirsty. 'Something should be done about it.'

Bill Cox said much the same thing a little later as he and his three juniors walked up to the unit together. 'You must go off early today, Tansy, lass,' he decreed.

'Mrs Dewar'll not like that, Bill.'

'You do as you're told and leave Mrs Dewar to me,' he ordered as they separated to their various wards.

The patients noticed her weariness. 'I reckon I should get out of this bed and let you have a bit of a lie-down, lass,' joked Mr Downie, after which the patient in the next bed said if it was him he'd not be getting out — just moving over. Tansy rose as required by telling him he was the cheekiest man she'd ever met, thus giving both men the laugh they'd been angling for.

Sister wasn't on duty that morning, as evidenced by the relaxed and smiling way the nurses were going about their work.

'No, I've no idea where she is,' said Staff when appealed to. 'Mind you, she has been having a lot of abdominal pain lately, so perhaps she's having another attack.'

Mollie asked if Sister had seen a surgeon, but Staff couldn't say, though she doubted it. 'Surely you've noticed that Sister always knows best, Doctor?' she asked wryly.

Sister wasn't the only one missing that morning. Struan hadn't shown up yet either. Tansy glanced at the clock and saw it was only half-past nine. She'd thought it was much later. Because I'm tired and want the morning over, she supposed.

She eventually saw him when she crossed over to the women's ward. He was pulling the curtains round Mrs Mitchell's bed. The bossy wee nurse who had questioned Tansy the day before was dancing attendance.

Mrs Carswell was two beds further along, and by the time Tansy had cleared her chest and taken her through deep breathing exercises Struan had completed his examination of Mrs Mitchell. They left the ward together. 'You've had a heavy night,' he said.

'I wonder how you know that?' asked Tansy, stifling a yawn.

'Because you look absolutely all in. Come into the doctors' room and I'll make you a coffee.'

'I'd love that, Struan, but I've got so much to do.'

'Doctor's orders,' he said, looking very determined. 'Besides, I want to tell you what we're planning for our new patient.'

'Yes, sir,' said Tansy, not at all sorry to be overruled.

'I love it when you're meek,' he said, opening the door for her. 'Sit there,' he ordered, pointing to the only armchair.

'But this is Dr Tait's chair.'

'He's at the Southern this morning, so he'll not be wanting it.'

Tansy collapsed gratefully where directed. 'I only hope I can get up again,' she murmured.

'If you can't, I'll be delighted to help,' said Struan, stooping down to kiss her gently. 'Poor little love,' he crooned. 'You really are exhausted. Something simply must be done about physio hours of work.'

'The senior staff are putting some statistics together with improvements in mind.'

'Splendid. And tell them they can count on the

medical staff for support.' He handed Tansy her coffee.
'Have you seen Mrs Mitchell at all?'

'Yes, I did an assessment yesterday afternoon. She's
in an acute phase, is she not?'

'Very much so. Her ESR is 124 and her haemoglobin
level at rock-bottom. That's why I admitted her. The
boss hasn't seen her yet, but my guess is he'll order
strict bed-rest for four weeks, plus a course of cortisone
and intravenous iron.' His glance softened. 'So that's
one patient who'll not be needing physio just yet.'

'Will she not be having routine maintenance exercises, then?'

'I hope not. It's my opinion that they settle quicker
without. What's your experience?'

'I haven't got any. We didn't all get a chance to work
on Rheumatology as students, and Kirsty and I missed
out.'

'Then it will be my pleasure to fill in that particular
gap for you.' Struan sat on the arm of her chair and
gave her a little hug.

'Struan! Remember where we are.'

'I know exactly where we are, sweetie, but the
archdragon is not here today. You'll be too tired to go
out tonight, I'm thinking,' he went on tenderly, his eyes
scanning her pale face.

'Oh, I don't know. . .' she began doubtfully.

'Well, I do, so I'm coming round to cook something
simple and when we've eaten you can send me home as
early as you like. How does that sound?'

'Wonderful — for me — but not exactly exciting for
you.'

'Being with you is always exciting, even when you're
as tired as you are today,' he insisted.

Tansy believed him. How could she possibly doubt
when he looked at her as he was doing now? She

drained her cup and stood up. 'You're such a dear,' she said huskily, leaning down to kiss the top of his curly head. 'But I must get on now that I'm refreshed. I'm really looking forward to tonight,' she added on a whisper.

'So am I,' he was saying when Mollie came in to say sorry, but she was having difficulty setting up that intravenous saline drip he'd ordered, and would he be a darling and come and bale her out?

At lunchtime, Bill told Tansy she was to be off the unit by three o'clock or he'd know the reason why. 'I wish I could give you the whole afternoon off, sweetie, but I'll not be free to take over from you much before that, I'm afraid.'

'Mrs Dewar——'

'Will be at a meeting in Admin, so she need never know.'

Much later, Tansy was to wonder how things would have turned out if she'd gone straight home, instead of deciding it wouldn't take much more than half an hour to go round by Jenner's and collect the casserole dish she'd ordered for Kirsty's birthday. And that was what she did, knowing it was the only chance she had of getting it in time. The shops always closed before she could get away on normal working days.

Tansy collected her parcel. Going back down the main staircase, she stopped dead, clutching at the banister rail. She had just seen Jean Norton going into the coffee-shop with Struan—and his arm was around her shoulders.

She was being silly. She was tired and her eyes were playing tricks on her. She went on down the stairs and headed for the exit.

But that picture was burning her brain. She stopped. Surely there was no harm in checking. . .

From the doorway of the coffee-shop she had a clear view of Struan and Jean sitting side by side. He was holding both her hands in his, and even as Tansy watched in disbelief her head drooped sideways on to his shoulder.

Instantly, Tansy was consumed by a tidal wave of anger that threatened to choke her. She could only think of one thing. Struan had pretended that all was over between him and Jean, but it wasn't. He was still seeing her — and they were still on excellent terms by the look of it. She had given him her trust and he had betrayed it, just as his brother had done. They were two of a kind after all, and only a silly, naïve little fool would ever have believed otherwise.

Tansy turned and stumbled towards the entrance again, bumping into people in her haste to get out of the shop. It was a miracle that she got on the right bus, but, having done so, she sat staring miserably ahead at nothing, clutching Kirsty's present tightly, her only link with reality.

That late-night meeting in the office of Ward Twenty was taking on a more sinister aspect now. He'd said he was counting on seeing *her* that night, but it was Jean who'd had his attention — not her. God, but he was devious! And so convincing. He'd really fooled her on Monday night — and again this morning. Tansy shivered when she thought how near she'd come to making the same mistake twice. And with Calum's twin too. There couldn't be many girls as stupid as she.

The bus shuddered to a halt, sending the standing passengers lurching and rousing Tansy from her trance. She peered through the steamy window and realised she'd gone past her stop. 'Excuse me — sorry, yes. I

know—sorry. . .' She half fell on to the pavement,
wrenching her ankle as the bus gathered speed again.
She limped painfully home, her mind still frantic. Oh,
yes, she could guess exactly why Struan had started
chatting her up. He and Jean would have had a quarrel,
but now they'd made it up—and so she was to be
disposed of. That really hurt, so she repeated it. She
was disposable—for Struan, as she had been for Calum.

All that sweet talk had been nothing but lies! And to
think *she* had been worrying about how Struan would
feel when he found out about Calum. What a fool she'd
been. What a complete and utter fool.

The minute she got home, Tansy undressed, took a
bath, and went to bed. Why not? Struan certainly
wouldn't be coming round now. Not now he'd patched
things up with his precious Jean.

Thank heaven Kirsty was going straight out to the
new house again tonight. She could wallow in misery
undisturbed. But Tansy was tired as well as miserable
and, after a night without sleep, fatigue soon won
through and she drifted off into an uneasy, troubled
doze.

She was roused by the persistent ringing of the
doorbell. She struggled awake, feeling around for the
light switch. When she opened the door she was yawning and pushing the hair out of her eyes. Then she
froze, her mouth hanging open. Struan was standing on
the mat with a bulging carrier from Marks and Spencer
in one hand and a Jenner's package in the other. His
expression was warm and eager. He held out the
package. 'Something to cheer you up, my darling,' he
said. 'I asked Kirsty what was your favourite perfume
and she said. . .' He stopped, puzzled by her stiff
posture and hostile eyes. 'Darling, what——?'

'What do *you* want?' she demanded harshly.

'Tansy—sweetheart. . . What's the matter?'

'What do you think?' she demanded satirically.

'I think you're behaving very oddly, and frankly, it worries me.' He came in, slamming the door shut with his shoulder. 'Look, it's me—Struan.' He put down his parcels and held out his arms.

'Oh, I know who you are,' she said bitterly. 'I'm just surprised to see you, that's all. In the circumstances.'

'What's that supposed to mean?' he demanded.

'You've come round to tell me in person, then. I didn't expect that. But I know already, as it happens.' Her voice was icy.

'Know what? Tansy, stop this! You're driving me crazy!' He advanced another step and tried to seize her but she eluded him.

'I know that I've outlived my usefulness. I'm no longer needed. I'm disposable!'

'For God's sake, Tansy, tell me in plain English what this is all about.' He looked and sounded utterly perplexed and troubled, and if she hadn't the evidence of her own eyes he would surely have convinced her.

'Bill Cox sent me off early today and I didn't come straight home. You're not the only one who's been to Jenner's today. I went there too and I saw you having coffee with—her. Or perhaps it was tea. I wasn't near enough to see!'

He'd certainly got the message now, but, instead of the blustering self-justification she'd been expecting of Calum's twin, Struan asked with tremendous self-control, 'Then why did you not join us?'

'You'd have liked that, I'll bet!'

'I'd certainly have preferred it to all this hysteria.'

That did it. Tansy flew at him, hammering his chest with her fists. 'That's right, make out I'm the one who's in the wrong, you—you double-dealing snake! Telling me you'd done with her—and dating us both! Well, nobody treats me that way—nobody! You hear? Let me go, you brute—you're hurting me!' she spat. He had taken her by the wrists and was forcing her arms down to her sides.

They glared at one another for several seconds before Struan said in a voice that throbbed with passion, 'I don't know whether you expect me to grovel and plead, but I'm not going to. You saw something which you misinterpreted. Think about it—get it in context. And then we'll talk.'

Even then things might have turned out differently if only she had calmed down. But she couldn't; she hadn't the confidence. Being scorned by both brothers was just too much to take. 'Oh, very clever! Make me out to be the one in the wrong,' she taunted. 'But I wasn't born yesterday. I've met your sort before. Have two, have ten—have twenty girlfriends if you like. Just don't expect me to be one of them!'

Struan released her so roughly then that she staggered back against the wall. 'I don't expect anything of the sort,' he said bitterly. 'That's not what I had in mind at all. I was besotted enough to think that we had something special, but I was wrong. If we had, you'd have trusted me instead of flying off the handle like that. Thank God I found you out before any lasting damage was done!' Then with one more scornful look that cut her to the heart, he marched out of the flat, and out of her life.

Tansy went and sat on her bed with her knees drawn up to her chin and her arms wrapped round them. The cheek of the man—coming round here and making out it was all her fault. And she'd thought he was different!

Well, so he was in a way. Where Calum had blustered and stormed when found out, Struan had gone for controlled dignity. But the result was the same. In both cases, she was to blame for objecting to their cheating. 'I should have known,' she moaned. 'I should have known it couldn't last. The whole damn thing was impossible from the start.'

CHAPTER NINE

KIRSTY didn't come home that night, which was both a relief and a problem — a relief because no Kirsty meant no need for painful explanations before she'd got herself together, a problem because Kirsty was invariably the first to wake and get moving. Tansy forgot to set her alarm, slept in, and was later for work than she'd ever been. Creeping nervously on to the ward, she couldn't decide whom she dreaded seeing most — Struan or Sister Aitken.

It was Staff Nurse Clarke who was sitting at the office desk again. 'But Sister never takes her days off during the week,' was Tansy's reaction.

'Needs must,' said Staff. 'She's going to Theatre today for a laparotomy.'

'The poor old thing — I didn't know she was ill.'

'Not many people did. All the nurses thought she was suffering from chronic digestion brought on by sheer bad temper, but she went to see Mr Shand yesterday morning and he ordered her in right away.'

'She could be off some time, then.' Even in her present state of 'all is lost', Tansy couldn't help cheering up a bit at the thought of somebody else in charge of Ward Eighteen.

'Yes, it's an ill wind,' returned Staff gleefully, only to look guilty next minute. 'That was an awful thing to say. Please ignore it, Tansy.' She reached for the card index and flicked through it. 'No changes to report among your flock, but I did hear Dr McLeod saying

something to Mollie about resting splints for Mrs
Mitchell, but he'll be telling you about those himself.'

Not if he can avoid it, guessed Tansy, as she thanked
Staff and left the office.

But she was wrong about that. As she passed the
open door of the doctors' room, Struan stepped out
into the corridor and called crisply after her, 'Do you
have a moment, please, Tansy?'

She halted, turning slowly. 'Yes, I suppose so,' she
muttered unwillingly, in marked contrast to his assured
detachment. If she needed confirmation that their quarrel hadn't hit him as hard as it had her, then this was it.

'Mrs Mitchell should have resting splints made for
wrists, knees and ankles,' he told her across the six feet
of tiled floor separating them.

'Yes. I'll see to it.'

'You know the kind Dr Tait favours, then?'

'No — but Bill Cox will.'

'If you're too busy, I could ask the plaster-room
technicians, but they are fairly busy too.'

'I'll see to it,' Tansy repeated woodenly.

'Thank you,' he answered coolly before going into
the room again and shutting the door.

That encounter had left her in a sorry state. Her
heart was pounding away at a rate too fast to count and
she could hardly swallow for the lump in her throat.
Yet he had shown no embarrassment at all. It wasn't
fair.

'You feeling all right, hen?' asked the motherly
cleaner who'd been energetically mopping the corridor.

'Eh? Oh, yes — fine, thanks.' Hastily Tansy
reassembled her protective armour. 'Just wondering
how to fit everything in today.'

'You and me both,' said the woman. 'So good luck
to ye, then.' The electric mop resumed its whirring.

I mustn't be caught out like that again, resolved Tansy as she speeded up and practised a cheerful smile for Mr Downie.

She forgot the smile as soon as she saw him. He looked very ill, lying back on his pillows with his eyes closed and his complexion grey. Tansy seized his left wrist, feeling for the pulse. She could only just detect it and his hand was cold and clammy. 'You've got a pain in your chest!' she exclaimed anxiously.

He opened his eyes and asked weakly. 'How did ye ken that?'

'I guessed!' Tansy ran out of the ward to find Staff and blurt out her fears. Staff was on her feet in an instant, running to find a doctor.

Tansy headed for the women's ward, where Mrs Carswell was her next most acute chest case. 'And are *you* feeling all right today?' she asked of that lady.

Mrs Carswell looked surprised. 'Yes, fine, thanks, love, but you're not looking so hot yourself.'

Fat lot of good I am, thought Tansy. It's come to something when the patients I should be reassuring start worrying about me. 'I'm fine—just a bit over-anxious. . .'

'You take your work too seriously,' decided the patient. 'But better that than the other way, I'm thinking. You'll need to fetch me another sputum carton before we start, though. I've nearly filled this one already,' she added with pride.

'My goodness, you have been busy! I'll soon be redundant at this rate,' exclaimed Tansy, trotting out a well-worn joke.

'Not till we've all learned to up-end ourselves and batter the deep stuff out of the corners,' returned Mrs Carswell, conjuring up a comical picture of self-administered postural drainage.

'There! What did I tell you?' she demanded when Tansy's judicious pummelling had produced some more. 'Though why ever you chose to do this for a living, I'll never know.'

'But do you feel better for it?' asked Tansy.

'Oh, yes, but——'

'There you are, then. I like to be useful, Mrs Carswell.'

'You're an angel,' Mrs Carswell was saying when Struan reached her bed on his usual morning mini-round. He pulled back the curtains. 'And here comes another one,' she added.

'Another what—another pest?' he asked with a crooked smile.

She looked very shocked. 'Oh, Doctor, what a thing to say! I was just telling our wee physio here that she's an angel.'

Struan turned and eyed Tansy from head to toe and back. 'I shouldn't think that's something you're often told, Miss Nicholson,' he observed coolly as he unwound his stethoscope and advanced on the patient.

Tansy backed away. She knew a dismissal when she met one.

Mollie Findlay had just finished taking all the morning blood samples. 'Care for a coffee, Tansy?' she asked as Tansy shot past.

Tansy halted and said that was a marvellous idea, but so far she'd only managed to treat one patient and she ought to get her chests finished first. 'But I would like to know what you made of Mr Downie,' she added.

'A cardiac episode of moderate severity,' said Mollie, 'so he's for transfer to the coronary care unit for monitoring. Well spotted, that girl.'

'Not really—it was obvious, but I just happened to be the one who went to him at the right moment,' disclaimed Tansy. 'Now of course his heart will take priority.'

'Just so. There's no such thing as an uncomplicated medical condition outside the textbooks,' sighed Mollie. 'Still, keeping his chest clear will be a headache for some other poor physio now.'

'So it will,' realised Tansy. 'I'll miss him, though. He always cheers me up.'

Unlike you, she thought, as she stopped at the foot of Mrs Muir's bed. She forced a smile and asked, 'How are you today, Mrs Muir?'

'Mustn't grumble,' sighed that lady, going on to do just that. 'I've just got comfortable—well, almost—and now I s'pose you want me to cough and spit. It's wicked.'

Tansy produced her stethoscope. 'Only if necessary. I'll have a little listen first.'

She needed treatment, of course—as she was a chronic bronchitic it was inevitable—but she liked to think there was a chance of getting away with it. 'I manage fine at home without all this palaver,' she said grumpily.

'But you've got an acute chest infection now.'

'I know that—that's why I'm here.'

It was a relief to complete her treatment and move on to the next patient, an old hand at this game who knew almost more about the drill than Tansy did herself.

Knowing that Bill had a ward round that morning, Tansy waited until lunchtime to tackle him about splints for Mrs Mitchell. 'I hope you've not got a heavy date planned for tonight, Tansy,' he returned teasingly. 'That's a good two hours' work your boyfriend has given us.'

Tansy didn't bat an eyelid. 'No, no date, Bill.' Not

tonight—not ever again. . . She nearly lost her cool then. 'Tell me what we need. . .' she said quickly.

He reeled off a list of requirements, then said, 'We'll work in the treatment-room on your ward, and I'll try to get to you by four. OK?'

'Thanks, Bill.' It would mean working late again, but as Sister Aitken wasn't here there'd be nobody to tick her off.

Poor old Sister! She'll not be feeling at all fierce today, thought Tansy as she went back to work.

First, though, she called in at the office to see if there was any news. 'Not yet,' said Staff. 'She's not due in Theatre until two.' Staff pushed a cardboard box across the desk. 'We thought we ought to get her a few flowers. Heaven knows you've no reason to feel sorry for her, but. . .'

Tansy was already pulling her purse out of her pocket. 'Will a pound do? I'm a bit short this week.'

'Nobody is putting in more than fifty pence, so take some change.' Staff looked appealingly across the desk. 'I suppose you wouldn't volunteer to come with me when I visit her tomorrow?'

Tansy's eyes widened with amazement. 'But she hates me.'

'She hates everybody except that niece of hers. So what about it? None of the student nurses is keen and I'd hate to go alone. . .'

It was hard to resist such a desperate appeal. 'OK, why not?' sighed Tansy. 'Anyway, it's not likely we'll be allowed to stay.'

'You're a gem, Tansy,' said the staff nurse warmly, just as Struan and Mollie came in.

'I'm just going,' said Tansy, edging round him to get out of the little room.

'We've just been checking on Mr Downie,' he told her impassively.

'Oh, yes. . .' Tansy cleared her throat. 'How is he?'

'As well as can be expected. It was fortunate that you happened along when you did.'

'I suppose so. . .' And now tell me I did well— please!

'Have you made those splints yet?' he demanded curtly.

Tansy blinked. 'N-no. Bill can't help me until later on. We're very busy.'

'Then please forgive me for holding you up,' Struan retorted smoothly.

'That's all right. I mean. . .' But what did she mean? Tansy stumbled out, hot, humiliated and acutely conscious of Mollie and Staff Clarke both looking curious. She understood now why some of the girls were so reluctant to get involved with men they worked with. It was all right when things were going well, but all wrong and very embarrassing when it all blew up in your face.

There was no time for mooning, though; she must be cheerful and encouraging for her afternoon patients. And she must have everything ready for making those splints before Bill came.

'Did I forget anything?' she asked eagerly when he finally appeared.

Bill looked round the treatment-room. 'Bandages, stockinette, scissors. . . Only the patient, as far as I can see,' he teased. 'So wheel her in, Tansy.'

Mrs Mitchell wasn't at all sure she wanted to be 'weighed down by all that concrete', as she put it.

Patiently, Bill explained the importance of total rest for joints that were as painful and inflamed as hers, promising to eat his words if she wasn't almost pain-free by this time next week. Then he persuaded her to turn on to her face so that he and Tansy could mould the wet plaster-of-Paris bandages into supporting shells for her legs and feet. That done, they were gently eased off and laid aside to harden. Next, they sat her up again to make splints for her wrists and fingers. 'They look like table tennis bats,' said Mrs Mitchell, who had been partially reassured by Bill's explanation.

'If you think they'll serve the purpose, then you can try them out when you get home,' joked Bill. 'These things need twenty-four hours to dry out, so we'll have the final fitting tomorrow at the same time. OK?'

'If you say so, Mr Cox,' agreed the patient. Very few of them could resist Bill at his most persuasive.

'Did they not teach you in college that the power of persuasion is the physio's greatest weapon?' he asked when Tansy said as much. 'I mean, would you want to do some of the things we have to ask of our patients?'

'Like deep breathing and coughing the day after an abdominal op—or moving a painful joint because it'd seize up altogether if left until the pain was away? No, I would not!'

'Two very good examples,' he approved. 'Sorry I can't stop and help to clean up this mess, but I've a couple of ventilator cases to see some time—like half an hour ago.' He was away on the instant and Tansy frowned at all the mess they'd made. There was no tidy way of working with plaster of Paris.

She had cleaned the plastic sheeting and wiped down the tiled walls, and was on her hands and knees swabbing the floor when she sensed that somebody was watching from the doorway. She looked up to see Struan surveying her inscrutably. 'There's a mop somewhere for that,' he said.

Tansy was vividly reminded of the day he'd advised her to mop this very floor before Sister saw all the spilled ice. She swallowed and said, 'Sister doesn't like us to use it when plaster's involved. She says we never wash it out properly afterwards.'

'Sister is not here,' he said.

'But the cleaners don't like it either.'

The corners of his mouth took a downward turn. 'The question that occurs to me is why you should be doing this at all. It's a dreadful waste of treatment time,' he stated, marching off before she could answer.

Tansy would have liked to think he was indignant on her behalf, but his cool, detached manner denied that. That makes four times we've run into one another today, she realised. That was something of a record. It was ironic it should happen now, yet seldom before.

When Tansy eventually got home that evening, she found Kirsty and Hamish having supper in the kitchen. 'You're cutting it fine,' said Kirsty when Tansy opened the door.

Tansy eyed her in genuine bewilderment, having forgotten that Kirsty didn't know yet about the split with Struan.

Kirsty cast a look of amazement up at the ceiling. 'Was there ever a girl so blasé?' she asked. 'Struan's only taking her to the Pheasant tonight—and she's left herself about ten minutes to get ready.'

'Not every girl needs two hours to make herself pretty, sweetheart,' teased Hamish, earning himself a swipe with a rolled-up newspaper. 'All the same, you'd better get a move on, Tans,' he advised. 'Old Struan is great on the punctuality.'

'You've lost count,' Tansy said jerkily. 'That was supposed to be last night.'

'What do you mean—supposed to be?' Kirsty asked sharply. 'The roads were clear.'

'We didn't go. I was—too tired.'

'Yes, of course you would have been. She had a terrible night duty on Tuesday-Wednesday,' Kirsty explained to Hamish. 'And as Struan must be on tonight, I guess it's tomorrow, then?' she asked on a questioning note.

'It's off.' Tansy turned and ran to her room.

Inevitably Kirsty followed. 'What's happened?' she asked anxiously.

'It's all over. Finished. He's still seeing Jean Norton and doesn't mean to give her up.'

'I don't believe it!' What Kirsty really meant was that she didn't want to.

'Perhaps you will when you hear this,' said Tansy in the same stilted way she'd been using all along. Then she told Kirsty how she'd seen them together in Jenner's yesterday afternoon, and how Struan had subsequently refused to explain. 'He insisted that I should have trusted him — and put all the blame on me. Just as his precious brother did. I saw red and completely lost my temper.'

'And quite right too! So it seems they are two of a kind after all. And yet. . .' Kirsty fumed to a stop. Her fury on her friend's behalf was at war with her innate belief in Struan's sincerity. 'Oh, Tans! Is it really so? You're quite sure?'

'Of course I'm sure! It's all over — and judging by the way he's been today, he's glad!'

'And I had such high hopes. . . Hamish will be furious!' cried Kirsty, rushing out to tell him what she thought of his friend.

Tansy dropped disconsolately on to her bed. She should have known it was too much to hope that Kirsty wouldn't fly straight to Hamish when she was incapable of keeping anything from him. Next second, she heard his howl of disbelief, then Kirsty's voice raised too as they debated and condemned—and queried and wondered.

Ten minutes later, Kirsty was back with some supper on a tray. 'Good thing I cooked too much,' she said gruffly.

'Thanks, love, but I'm not hungry.'

'Nonsense! You had no lunch. . .' Kirsty hovered worriedly. Tansy thought, Please don't let her hug me, or I'll howl. . . 'Just give me five minutes alone with him,' Kirsty burst out. 'Him and his precious brother. Five minutes and I'd. . . I'd. . .' But not even Kirsty's buoyant personality was equal to this. 'Oh, hell,' she muttered and rushed out.

Tansy ate her mince and veg because not to would only set Kirsty off again, but it tasted like ashes.

Thanks to the Mogadon capsules Hamish insisted he just happened to have in his pocket, Tansy slept long and deeply that night. Such welcome oblivion almost made worthwhile the inevitable wooziness and apathy next morning.

'Now remember you're going to act sophisticated and as if nothing had happened,' urged Kirsty later, at the hospital, when they parted to go to their respective wards.

'No problem,' returned Tansy. 'I feel as though I've been anaesthetised.' And long may it last, she added to herself.

Staff Clarke, Mollie and Struan were all in the office, discussing Sister Aitken's operation. Tansy stood there, waiting to be noticed. When she caught Struan's eye she asked with perfect calm, 'Are there any new patients for me today, please, Struan?'

Her self-possession surprised him and, if she hadn't known about Jean, Tansy might have thought he was also disappointed. 'Just the one,' he said, sounding less assured than usual.

'Two, Struan,' corrected Mollie. 'There's also last night's emergency admission, don't forget.'

'Er — yes — the peppery old colonel. He has an acute chest infection superimposed on severe chronic bronchitis. There is also a history of asthma, so use your discretion about postural drainage.' He was into his stride now, sounding more confident and increasingly impersonal. 'Mrs Walker was admitted yesterday for stabilisation of her warfarin dosage. That doesn't concern you, but she also has severe osteoarthrosis of the right knee joint with loss of extension and gross weakness and wasting of quadriceps muscles. See what you can do for her, will you?'

'Of course I will. It'll make a nice change from treating respiratory and neurological disorders,' Tansy added impressively. Kirsty would have been delighted with her. 'May I take it the referral cards are in your room?'

'No, they're in my pocket,' admitted Mollie, producing them.

'Thank you. I'm off to get started now.' I handled that really well, she thought complacently. I wonder how long a Mogadon hangover lasts? Till after Staff and I have been sick-visiting, I hope. . .

Calling the new chest patient 'peppery' had been an understatement. 'I've had an X-ray, enough pills to cure an elephant, and yes, my bowels are working well,' barked Colonel Campbell as Tansy approached. 'So kindly go away, young woman!'

'But have you had your FEV measured?' she asked sweetly, producing the little gadget which patients often likened to a canister of confetti.

As she had hoped, curiosity got the better of the old

boy, and in his determination to blow away this latest nuisance he breathed out so hard that he began to cough. Tansy took out a specimen bottle and caught a sample for the lab. 'Hell's bells,' he said afterwards. 'That's no way for a girl to earn a living.'

'If it wasn't me bothering you, it would be somebody else. Now I'm going to measure your chest expansion.'

'If I had my way, women would be kept in their place,' he growled. Tansy didn't rise. She'd met his sort before and knew you just couldn't win. This was one for Bill's list.

The women could talk of nothing else that morning but Sister's operation. 'Yes, yes, my chest is fine,' insisted Mrs Carswell, 'but have you heard how Sister is?'

Tansy said no, not yet.

Mrs Strachan was almost tearful. 'If I'd known the puir soul was ill, I'd never have said what I did about her being the next to get a stroke,' she sighed.

For Tansy's money, a stroke would have been the likeliest option, but she couldn't say so. 'Anybody can be wise after the event,' she comforted, thinking that Sister would probably be better before Mrs Strachan recovered from her stroke. 'Right now, into the ice bath with that hand,' she said bracingly. 'That's the way, swirl it about. Now try to open your fingers— splendid!'

'Why is it that icing helps your fingers when you've had a stroke, yet they go all numb and won't work if you go out without gloves in the cold weather?' asked Mrs Strachan.

Now there was a question! Tansy took a deep breath to tackle it when Mrs Barr chimed in with, 'It's all to do with the reflexes, and the spasm and that. You remember! Miss Alford told us all about it after she'd read that book.'

'Of course,' agreed Mrs Strachan, not wanting to be thought slower on the uptake than her new friend.

Tansy was saved. There was no way to explain the complex workings of the brain and nervous system as easily as, say, the workings of a joint. Patients with neurological conditions had to take so much more for granted.

They took Sister her flowers immediately after lunch. 'Then she can't accuse us of neglecting our work,' said Staff.

'Side-room four—and only five minutes, mind,' said the sister in charge. 'She's very weak.'

Weak or not, she gave them a tremendous frown and a 'Well, what's this, then?' until she saw the flowers. 'Very nice,' she allowed then. 'I'll have them beside the roses from my niece and Dr McLeod.' That was said with a complacent look for Tansy.

Tansy took it on the chin and leaned forward to smell the roses. 'Mmm, lovely—and such a beautiful colour,' she observed calmly.

But never had five minutes seemed so long. Staff was kept on the hop, plumping up pillows, adjusting the window, and putting Sister's chart where she could read it, but there was nothing for Tansy to do but stand there and think about the significance of those roses.

On the way out, they met Struan and Jean Norton coming in. She's leaning on him as though she's the one who's had the op, thought Tansy waspishly, while producing a smile and a cheery 'Good afternoon, you two.'

Jean shot Tansy a glance of sheer triumph, while Struan looked both annoyed and acutely embarrassed.

As well he might, after all that waffle about her lack of trust!

Staff turned round and gazed thoughtfully after them. 'Now there's a lassie who's milking this situation for all she's worth,' she observed acutely. 'Sister dotes on her, but Jean Norton's never bothered much with her aunt — until now.'

Tansy had been thinking along similar lines but her answer was generosity itself. 'She and Struan McLeod are old friends,' she said. 'She'll be grateful for his — support at a time like this.'

'If they're not old friends, you can take it from me that it's not her fault,' Staff answered tartly. 'She's been pursuing him relentlessly ever since he set foot in the place. She's not much liked, you know. All the night staff on Twenty were hoping that you would cut her out.'

'So sorry to disappoint,' said Tansy. 'If I'd known that, I'd have tried harder.' Had that sounded as humorous as she'd intended? Probably not; that was a very funny look Staff was giving her. Oh, yes, this would be the last time she got involved with a colleague.

When Tansy bustled into the women's ward soon after, Mrs Carswell cowered back against her pillows and pulled the covers up to her chin, feigning terror. 'My, but you're looking fierce,' she said. 'I hope I'm not next.'

Tansy thrust aside her personal concerns and made a big effort. 'I'm saving you for the grand finale,' she claimed. 'It's Mrs Walker who's for the high jump now.'

'I hope you don't mean that,' said the patient, entering into the fun. 'Otherwise you'll need to lend me a trampoline.'

'Not before this time next week,' promised Tansy,

keeping the fun going. 'Right now, let's see what's to
be done here.'

'Not a lot, I should think,' sighed Mrs Walker,
throwing off the cover to reveal a grossly swollen joint
which looked thicker than the wasted thigh above it.

'I never could resist a challenge,' claimed Tansy not
altogether truthfully as she fished in her pocket for her
tape-measure.

'That's my good one,' pointed out the patient when
Tansy slipped it under her left knee.

'Just checking to see what we're aiming at,' Tansy
explained. Good grief! The right knee was blown up by
four inches, almost as much as the extensor muscles
lacked in bulk. This was no ordinary example of a
lifetime's wear and tear. 'You've injured this knee at
some time,' she assumed.

'Aye, coming off my bike didn't do much for it. And
right in the path of that bus, too. . .'

Tansy stifled a sigh. 'Now I'm not making any prom-
ises,' she began, 'but it should be possible to ease the
pain and loosen the joint up a bit.' She rolled up a
pillow and placed it under the swollen knee. 'Let's try
tightening these muscles. That's the way—keep your
knee pressed down on the pillow and lift your foot as
high as it will go. . .'

I could kill you, Struan McLeod, thought Tansy as
she left Mrs Walker to make her last round of the
chests for the day. What are you trying to do to me—
ruin my credibility as a therapist? You must know that
only a joint replacement is any use here. Yet another
reason for not getting involved with a colleague. It was
too damned easy for him to take revenge—even if he
was the one at fault.

Kirsty had taken a half-day's holiday to go and
choose carpets for the new home, so Tansy was waiting

alone at the bus-stop that night. A cruel east wind was gusting along the street, penetrating her anorak and whipping off the hood. She shivered and pulled it on again, tightening the draw-string around her face.

It was early March and the weather was like the middle of an Arctic winter, but Easter and Kirsty's wedding were only a month away now.

So far, Tansy had given little thought to the change that Kirsty's marriage would make to her own life, but soon she'd be going home alone every night. She'd also have to find a new flat-mate; she could never afford the rent without help.

Why did troubles never come one at a time? Losing Kirsty, losing Struan. . .

A vicious hailstorm suddenly descended. A stone struck Tansy's cheek, making her eyes water, and she was mopping up when a cheerful voice broke in on her concentration. 'Tansy! It is Tansy, is it not? You remember me—Catriona McLeod.'

'Yes, of course—sorry. I didn't notice you in this beastly storm. How are you?' I sound absolutely pathetic, Tansy thought crossly.

Catriona hadn't noticed. 'I'm fine now, thanks, but that was some flu bug I got.' She seemed to think Tansy would know all about her illness. What could Struan have said to his sister? 'But why are you waiting out here?' Catriona wondered. 'I'm sure Struan told me we were meeting in the car park at six.' She looked at the clock over the gate. 'What's keeping him, Tansy?'

Why is she so sure that I know his every move? 'I don't know, Catriona. He covers the whole medical unit—not just the ward I'm on.' She was praying that her bus would come before Struan drove out and found her talking to his sister. He might think she was trying to curry favour. . .

'Oh, great!' exclaimed Catriona when she saw his car. He stopped at the kerb beside them. 'You go in front,' said Catriona, giving Tansy a friendly shove.

Tansy hung back. For a wild moment, she thought of saying she was going in the opposite direction, but that wouldn't hold water when she was waiting on this side of the road.

'I don't care who goes where,' said Struan. 'Just get in, the pair of you, and shut the doors. It's perishing!'

By then Catriona was in the back and there seemed no alternative to accepting the lift, however grudgingly offered. Tansy got in beside Struan, muttering thanks.

'My pleasure,' he returned satirically as they pulled away from the kerb. Catriona hooted with laughter at that and told him he was an absolute scream.

Tansy was now more confused than ever. The only possible explanation for Catriona's attitude was that Catriona thought she was Struan's girlfriend. She supposed it was possible he'd told his sister he was taking her out, but how could she not know about Jean Norton — girlfriend number one? Perhaps she did, though — and admired her brother's versatility. After all, playing the field was the rule in their family.

'I do wish you two would talk,' complained Catriona from the back seat. 'You're making me feel like the proverbial gooseberry and I don't like it.'

'Perhaps we would — if you ever stopped,' retorted Struan, not entirely unreasonably.

At that, Catriona took the huff, and into the awkward silence ensuing Tansy eventually said, 'That's a truly terrible knee of Mrs Walker's.'

Struan snatched at the straw. 'The poor woman's been lame for years — ever since a road traffic accident in which she fractured both femoral condyles and the patella.'

'Yes, she said something about an accident,' Tansy persisted.

'Shop talk,' sighed Catriona. 'That's only just better than nothing. Now I feel more *de trop* than ever.'

No more than I do, thought Tansy. Fortunately it's only a short journey.

When Struan stopped the car at Tansy's door, his sister wiped the steam off the window and peered out. 'Where are we, then?' she demanded.

'This is where I live,' said Tansy, unfastening her seatbelt.

'But I thought you were coming round to Struan's place. He said——'

'No,' said Tansy shortly, opening the door. He was the one responsible for this misunderstanding, so let him resolve it. 'It was nice to see you again, Catriona. And thanks for the lift, Struan,' she added when he also got out and faced her across the car.

'I wouldn't leave a dog standing on the pavement in this weather,' he retorted in a voice pitched too low for his sister to hear.

'You're too kind—but then nobody is all bad. Or so it's said,' Tansy flung back at him before bolting for the shelter of the porch.

She fumbled her key into the lock, furious with herself for making such an inept and childish reply. Surely she could have come up with something better than that? But then both that meeting and the lift had been so unexpected. I'll do better next time, she promised herself. Next time, I'll be ready. I can't have him thinking I *mind*!

CHAPTER TEN

THE GIRL turned round on the doorstep and said, 'I think I should tell you that I've got a couple of cats — but they're mostly pretty good about using the tray. And I'm learning the trumpet, but as you're not a student I doubt that'd matter.'

Tansy had quite liked this one, but now her hopes were taking a nosedive as she trotted out the usual formula about others to see and letting her know. 'So I'll ring you as soon as possible,' she repeated as she shut the door.

Five since teatime, and none of them suitable. She went to take a bath, lying back in the warm, scented water to take stock.

It was early days yet. Kirsty had only moved out yesterday, taking her possessions to her new home before going north to Ullapool, to spend her last few days as a single girl with her parents. But none of the potential flatmates Tansy had interviewed on this blustery first Sunday in April had come within a mile of filling the void Kirsty had left behind.

And while on the subject of voids. . . But she had vowed to think no more of Struan Mcleod. Something was ended that should never have begun. It was galling, though, the impression he had been giving of complete indifference. But then he had Jean Norton, whereas she had nobody.

She had been slightly cheered at discovering that he hadn't taken Jean home with him when he had gone off so suddenly last Thursday, until she reflected that a

170

family gathering for his grandmother's funeral was hardly a suitable time for introducing the girlfriend.

Tansy shivered, and not only because the bath-water was getting cold. She'd been badly shaken when she had heard Struan telling Mollie that he was going home to Mull. This would be the first time Struan had seen his brother since he had met her — and now, surely, he must find out all about her affair with his twin. He would despise her more than ever and regret her even less.

How miserable she had been until she had started thinking rationally again. Then she had realised that she was firmly in the past for both brothers, so what possible reason could either of them have for even mentioning her name? She must have been crazy to imagine such a thing.

Tansy stood up and reached for her bath-towel. This was postively the last time she was going to think of either McLeod. From now on, she would look forward, not back. 'I wonder if I'll meet somebody nice at Kirsty's wedding?' she asked her reflection in the nearest mirror.

First things first, though. She had to set the alarm to make sure she got to work on time tomorrow. Kirsty had always been the first to stir. I should have included 'must be early riser' in that newspaper ad, she thought wryly.

Not that the occasional lapse was quite so critical now that nice Sister Alison Macaulay had taken over for the duration of Mighty Mouse's convalescence. At her operation, Mr Shand had found a large tumour. Though very difficult to remove, it had fortunately proved to be benign at biopsy, but the long operation had taken a lot out of her and she wouldn't be back to

work before Tansy moved on to Geriatrics at the end
of the month.

Next morning, Tansy went straight to the office for the
Monday morning update which Alison was always
happy to give. But this morning Alison had hardly got
started when Struan came in. 'Good morning,' he said,
actually including Tansy. 'And if that's a report you're
giving Miss Nicholson, please carry on, Sister. I need
an update too and it'll save you repeating yourself.'

'Are you not the thoughtful one?' laughed Alison.
'Now where was I?' She rounded off an expert resumé
of present states by concluding, 'So all your patients are
just that little bit better than when you left them on
Saturday, Tansy, so no problems there. However, we
had three new admissions yesterday. Mr Stobie is back
with a second left-sided stroke and is understandably
depressed. Mrs Veitch, who has acute exacerbation of
chronic bronchitis, is another old customer, I'm told.
The third patient is Mr Glen from Orthopaedics. That
unit is full to bursting, after that pile-up on the Glasgow
road following the Hearts and Celtic match on
Saturday, so they had to board out some of their stable
cases to make room for the casualties.'

'It sounds to me as though all the new ones will be
needing your attention,' said Struan to Tansy. 'I'll
check them over and let you know as soon as I can.'

'Thank you, Doctor,' said Tansy, sounding as surprised as she looked. She couldn't remember the last
time he'd spoken to her so spontaneously. 'And thank
you, Alison. I appreciate all the trouble you take.'

'It's all part of the job in my book,' Sister called after
her as Tansy left the office. 'What a conscientious wee
soul she is,' she added, but Tansy didn't manage to
catch Struan's low-voiced reply.

Chests first as usual. Mrs Rowan had been very reluctant to have physiotherapy, being under the impression that it was all to do with muscle-building and fancy electrical machinery. Not surprisingly, she hadn't been able to see how any of that would help her chest condition. But once Tansy had taught her to breathe more deeply, instead of gasping, and had shown her why coughing lying down was less tiring, Mrs Rowan became an enthusiast. And she adored having her forced expiratory volume measured. She called it being breathalysed, which was a pretty good parallel when you thought about it. 'Will you be reporting me if it turns green?' she asked this morning.

'Only if you go for a spin along Princes Street in your bed,' promised Tansy.

She had finished all her chest treatments and was wondering if she could possibly squeeze in a coffee-break before starting on the strokes, when Struan came up to her. 'About those new patients, Tansy,' he said. 'Have you got a moment?'

'Yes — of course.' She produced notebook and biro, but he was walking away, so she followed him out of the ward.

'I think Mollie's got the kettle on,' he said, ushering her into the doctors' room, surprising her some more.

There was no sign of Mollie, but the kettle was gently steaming. Struan made two mugs of instant coffee and handed one to Tansy. She took it with a muttered word of thanks. This was the first friendly gesture he'd made since their quarrel. He was looking at her, too, looking at and not through her as he'd always seemed to do of late.

She was suddenly acutely self-conscious. 'Those patients,' she blurted out.

'Oh, yes. The patients.' Had he really forgotten why

he'd led her here? 'Right, Mr Stobie first. You'll not remember him, but he was in the ward before Christmas with a transient left-sided hemiparesis, the typical early warning. We thought we had him well controlled, but now he's back with a profound hemiplegia and a blood-pressure that's practically through the roof. It's a harsh judgement, but I'm afraid he can't have been following the drugs regime we worked out for him. You'll not be able to do much in the way of active rehabilitation until his BP comes down, but you'll need to watch out that he doesn't develop contractures and so forth. Not that I need to remind you of that.' He frowned thoughtfully. 'He's very depressed and tearful, poor old chap.'

'But at least he's conscious.'

'Yes. I hope he makes it — he's got a devoted wife.'

'That's nice. It's always so heartening to see a loving old couple propping each other up.'

'Something for us all to aim at,' Struan returned drily. 'And now we come to Mrs Veitch. She's a real character — smokes sixty a day, says she always has and refuses to accept that's why she's a respiratory cripple. I don't envy you the task of emptying her lungs every morning.'

Encouraged by this return to conversation, however professional, Tansy ventured, 'That makes me sound like a — a medical refuse collector.'

Struan very nearly smiled at that. 'How very apt,' he agreed. 'But before I forget, I must warn you. Mrs Veitch is a bit of a warrior.'

'Heavy smokers usually are — they have to be, faced as they see it with prejudice on every side.'

'Make that common sense and concrete evidence and I'll agree with you,' he was replying when Mollie looked in to say the orthopaedic registrar was here and asking for him.

'He'll be here to see our boarder,' guessed Struan. 'Mr Glen has had multiple skin grafts to his right lower leg and needs thrice daily lanolin massage to keep them supple. I'd better go, but don't feel you have to hurry. Finish your coffee.'

What a remarkable change in attitude one long weekend had made! Tansy could hardly believe it, but she was reassured on one point. Whatever he and Calum had talked about, she had not been on the agenda. If she had been, Struan would now be even more morose than he had been before he had gone home. She was avid to see how he behaved the next time they met.

Before that, though, the collecting box appeared on Alison's desk. It was the first thing Tansy noticed when she looked in for her briefing next morning. Brought up to date, she then asked curiously, 'So who's ill or leaving or getting married this time, Alison?'

'Jean Norton, night staff nurse on Twenty,' Alison returned carelessly.

Tansy felt the floor lurching under her feet. When it settled, she asked with an effort, 'So when's it to be?'

'The end of the month.' Oh, no! So soon? Tansy gripped the edge of the desk. 'She'll probably earn twice as much,' said Alison, 'but she'll have to work three times as hard for her money.'

'You've — lost me,' Tansy breathed feebly.

'Jean Norton has landed herself a job at a rather famous hospital in Baltimore, USA.'

Tansy was so relieved that, had a chair been handy, she would have dropped down on to it. As it was, she perched on the desk while she opened her purse and took out a couple of pounds which she dropped in the box. 'It's a very big step, taking a job like that.'

'And quite unexpected, I gather.' Alison was a new girl at the Royal Alex. 'One can only speculate as to her reasons.'

You and me both, thought Tansy, who had been speculating like mad for the past two minutes. 'Let's hope it all works out well. You did say third side-room for Mrs Veitch, Alison?'

'That's right. We had to move her out of the big ward when she refused to stop smoking.'

'She's about the worst, so I think I'll begin with her this morning,' said Tansy, getting herself out of the office. But after that bombshell, she needed a minute or two to herself before beginning work. Why was Jean Norton leaving? Was this a previous arrangement, made before she met Struan? Or was she leaving because she could see she was getting nowhere with him? Surely the second possibility. If she was as keen on him as everybody thought, she'd have no compunction about breaking her contract and staying here—if he wanted her to.

And did her coming departure have anything to do with Struan's sudden change of attitude to herself? Well, what if it did? There was still the little obstacle of her affair with Calum. Nothing was changed.

So when a little later on Tansy came face to face with Struan again—and he suggested coffee—she told him very politely how kind that was of him, but she'd be lucky if she even got time for lunch that day.

He didn't exactly go out of his way to chat after that. Tuesday dragged by and then Wednesday, and now it was Thursday and her turn for a long weekend off.

Tomorrow, Hamish's brother David would be driving her up to Ullapool for the wedding. At least that was the plan. Tansy had just finished the early morning round of her chesty patients when Mollie called out that she was wanted on the phone in the doctors' room. Naturally Tansy expected a hospital call, but it was Hamish calling from Ullapool. 'Tansy? Glad I got you!' He sounded agitated. 'That brother of mine has landed up in Surgical at your place with a ruptured appendix. How's that for timing? He said to tell you not to worry, though, because you can borrow his car.'

Tansy let out a wail. 'His new Jag? Oh, Hamish, I couldn't possibly! I've never driven anything faster than a tractor—and my aunt's old Fiat. I'll get the train or a bus or whatever, but I'll get there somehow, don't you worry!'

'I told him you'd turn down the offer of the car,' said Hamish, 'but we can't have you coming by public transport. Apart from anything else, you'd probably not arrive in time. There's bound to be somebody driving up tomorrow who has room for one more. I'll ring round and get back to you, but first, could you find old Struan for me?'

'He's not on the ward just now, so hold on and I'll put you back to the switchboard. Give my love to the bride,' she remembered to say before effecting the transfer.

'Old Struan' indeed, she thought scornfully. Very matey. But then men always stuck together, didn't they? And to be fair, they were old friends—which was why Struan would almost certainly be going to the wedding!

Tansy was still trying to decide whether that was or was not a good thing when she met Struan on the stairs as she was going to lunch. She would have passed him with a brief smile and a nod, but he said, 'That's rotten luck about Hamish's brother.'

'Yes. Especially as he was to have been best man. I wonder whom Hamish will ask instead?'

'He's already appointed a substitute.'

'You're very well informed!' she exclaimed, thinking Hamish might have told her too.

'Naturally,' he said woodenly. 'I'm the substitute.'

She might have known! 'No wonder he was so keen to get hold of you.'

Struan folded his arms and looked down on her assessingly. 'He also mentioned that you are now without transport. . .'

'No, I'm not,' she said. 'I'm getting the train. I've made some enquiries and——'

'So you know that you'll not get there this side of midnight tomorrow, then.'

She couldn't refute that, not having rung the station yet. 'I love travelling, so don't you worry about me,' she said stoutly.

He stared her down without too much difficulty and then he said levelly, 'As far as I'm concerned you can turn up at the church on a motorbike if the fancy takes you. However, as best man, it's my duty to oversee the arrangements and I'm damn well going to see that you arrive in good time and in a fit state to play your part. I'll pick you up at nine on the dot tomorrow morning. So please be ready!' He climbed the rest of the stairs and disappeared before Tansy had recovered.

She got through the rest of the day in a dream, making the right noises and saying the right things, while her thoughts were all the time on what was to come. And what was to come? After their quarrel and with Struan apparently untroubled and occupied with Jean, it had been easy to persuade herself that she was glad it was over because the whole thing had been doomed from the start. But now Jean was out of the picture and Struan was sending out friendly signals once more. Even putting it no higher than that was alarming, when the merest look or smile of his could rekindle the flame he had lit in her. Because he had. She knew that now. He himself and as himself, not as a substitute for his brother whom he resembled in looks so exactly, but in character rather less.

'Not another treatment, Miss Nicholson?' protested Mrs Rowan when Tansy paused abstractedly by her bed. 'You've already been to me this afternoon.'

'Oh, help—so I have! Sorry, Mrs Rowan. But better too many visits than too few, though.'

'You've got too much to do—that's the trouble. And it's getting you down.'

'That's kinder than telling me I'm wool-gathering,' Tansy said gratefully.

'You—wool-gathering? Now there's a laugh. Who is coming to us while you're away to your friend's wedding, dear?'

'Mr Cox, I expect, but I'll be back on Monday.' After a second long drive with Struan on Sunday. Yes, there'd be two exposures. How come she'd overlooked that?

But perhaps he's taking somebody else as well as me, she thought as she let herself into the flat that night. Oh, please, let that be so. Otherwise. . .

When the black VW turned the corner into the Terrace next morning, Tansy was waiting at the kerbside with her luggage.

Struan sprang out to hoist it into the boot. 'I didn't know you were staying on,' he said.

'I'm not, but my dress needs a whole case to itself. So many flounces. . .' Which don't suit me. I'm too well-rounded. 'I should have told you I'd need two cases. Now there's no room for anybody else's stuff in the boot.'

'Who said anything about anybody else?' he asked when they were in the car and ready to go.

'I just wondered. . . After all, quite a lot of folk are going from Edinburgh.'

'But none of them with us,' said Struan.

She ought to be sorry about that. And she was, really. So why that silly little lift when he'd told her they'd be travelling alone? What an illogical little fool you are, she scolded herself.

'I'm sorry,' said Struan grimly, breaking in on her musings.

'What about?' she asked, puzzled.

'That you have to put up with me all the way to Ullapool.'

'I didn't mean——'

'I'm afraid you did. Perhaps I should have let you go by public transport after all.'

'No, I'm sure you were right—about it taking forever.' She might be mixed-up and basically miserable, but one thing Tansy was sure of. She didn't want to quarrel with him again if it could be avoided.

'Approximately twice as long as by car, actually. I checked.'

'Imagine that.' She waited until he had negotiated the busy junction at Toll Cross before adding, 'I should be very grateful.'

'I think so too.'

'And I am. It was only that I didn't—didn't want you to feel that you *had* to. Take me.' She couldn't leave it there, that two-word phrase had such erotic undertones. 'With you—all the way to Ullapool.'

'I think I get your point. And thanks for reminding

me where we're going. I just might have forgotten,'
Struan responded woodenly.

Tansy couldn't decide whether or not he was laughing
at her. The heavy traffic was excuse enough for not
talking as long as they were in the city, but, once
beyond Cramond and making for the Forth Road
bridge, the silence became embarrassing.

'I'm glad it's such a nice day,' said Tansy desperately.

'As long as it's a nice day tomorrow as well.'

'Yes, of course. But at this time of year — and in the
north-west. . .'

'Let's hope for the best,' he said.

The weather now exhausted as a topic, Tansy thought
of rummaging in her capacious handbag for her purse.
It was of course at the bottom.

'You can't possibly want to redo your face yet,' said
Struan when she dredged up her make-up bag.

'I'm trying to find my purse. To pay the bridge toll.'

'I've got it here.'

'But you must let me ——'

'Too late. We'll be there in five minutes.'

'There is nothing in this bag which I don't need,'
Tansy said dangerously.

'A man could go away for a week with a smaller one
than that,' Struan retorted.

'Only because he stuffs so much into his pockets!'

'What easier way to carry things? That bag must
weigh a ton. And that's very bad for your shoulders.'

'If there is one thing a physio knows, it's how to carry
weights.'

'I'd always understood that the idea was an equal
weight in either hand,' said Struan infuriatingly. 'At
least, that's what I've always heard.'

A girl'd look pretty silly with two handbags,' said
Tansy before she realised that was ceding the argument.

Tight-lipped, she went back to rummaging. Too late. He'd paid the toll.

Halfway across the bridge, they were honked at and waved to by a red Ford full of cheerful-looking young men and women, who indicated with a lot of arm-waving as they passed that they would be stopping at the next lay-by. Struan stopped behind them and ran forward to confer.

Doctor friends of Hamish's also on their way to the wedding, diagnosed Tansy. Struan confirmed that when he returned. 'We'll be meeting for coffee in Pitlochry,' he said.

'Not me,' denied Tansy, squirming at the thought of all the winks and innuendoes. 'If we're stopping in Pitlochry, then I shall go to MacNaughton's and buy a sweater.'

'That will really pad your bag out a treat,' said Struan as they set off again.

'You never give up, do you?' she threw at him.

'That rather depends on whether a project is worth pursuing,' he told her.

After that, she resolved not to speak again until spoken to. They went the rest of the way to Pitlochry in silence.

Tansy held to her resolve to go shopping instead of having coffee and she took so long over it that the red Ford had gone and Struan was drumming impatient fingers on the steering-wheel of the VW when she got back to the car park.

'I've kept you waiting,' she said unnecessarily.

'That's all right. We've only overrun the limit by ten minutes.'

'Only I saw this dear little kitchen clock which was just what Kirsty's been searching for, so I had to buy it. But the shop was full of foreign tourists buying souvenirs and arguing about VAT. And I couldn't get served.'

'So you didn't get it after all.'

'Yes, I did. In the end, I went up to the manager and I said, "I've been standing here for nearly half an hour and if you don't serve me this instant I shall walk out without paying." That did it.'

'I'll bet it did.' She saw his mouth twitching, but he managed not to smile. 'What a pity you can't bring such decision to bear on more important aspects of your life.'

'It all depends on whether a project is worth pursuing, don't you think?' she asked triumphantly.

She expected that would really melt the ice, but it didn't. With an indrawn hiss of breath, Struan launched the car out of the car park and on to the road, his expression dark.

Now what have I said? she wondered unhappily. He can't think I was referring to *us*. After all, he was the one who caused that quarrel by refusing to explain about Jean. And he *still* hasn't explained. I'd give a lot to know why she's going. . .

They went on past Killiecrankie, Blair Atholl and Calvine and into Glen Garry with nothing much said on either side. If he doesn't start a conversation soon, I'll scream, thought Tansy, as they caught up with a long stream of traffic crawling uphill behind a small car towing an over-large caravan. After a mile or two of that, with the engine beginning to overheat, Struan drove into a lay-by and switched off the ignition. 'I've had enough of this,' he growled.

'We're making good time,' she said. 'It's a good idea to let that lot get well ahead.'

'What time are we expected anyway?'

'Kirsty guessed we'd arrive somewhere about three when I phoned her last night.'

'Not at this rate, we'll not.' He sighed. 'The others will be miles ahead by now.'

'Because they didn't waste time at Pitlochry.'

'Partly,' said Struan.

There was a long pause after that, with Tansy looking away and out of the window all the time. And then he said suddenly, 'Hamish tells me that you and Kirsty have known each other a long time.'

His tone was conciliatory and seemed to warrant a reasonable reply. 'Yes, we went to the same school in St Andrews. I was a day girl, but she was a boarder. Her father was still in the Army then so her parents were constantly on the move. And then of course we trained together.'

'You're going to miss her.'

'I certainly am. And you're going to miss Jean.' Now why had she said that—introducing a controversial note just when they looked like having a civilised conversation?

She could feel Struan's questioning glance like a touch before he answered, 'Yes, I rather think I will. By and large, she's a very kind, cheerful, uncomplicated girl.'

Tansy wondered why he hadn't added, 'Unlike you,' when that was clearly what he meant. 'In that case, I'm very surprised that you're letting her get away,' she retorted tartly.

'I have no choice,' he said quietly. 'While we were just good friends, it was fine. But Jean wanted more and that I couldn't give. It would have been unkind and selfish to let her go on hoping.' When she didn't comment, he assumed, 'You don't agree.'

'Oh, yes I do,' said Tansy. 'But I was wondering

exactly when you made that sensible decision.' Before or after I saw you together in Jenner's? She finished in her mind.

'Why do you ask?'

She shrugged. 'Just curious. After all, there was a time. . .' She left it there, wishing she hadn't said as much.

'You can't leave it there,' Struan said quietly.

'Forget it. It's — none of my business.'

'In that case, why did we quarrel so violently about her?' he asked bluntly.

'Good question,' said Tansy while she tried to come up with an answer that wouldn't get her in deeper than she was already. Raking over old ashes was dangerous.

'Good questions require good answers,' he insisted.

'You know perfectly well why we quarrelled,' she said slowly at last. 'And when you refused to explain — well, naturally I thought my assumption was correct.'

'I understand that now. But at the time I was hurt and angry because you didn't trust me.'

'I suppose you were breaking it to her gently that you could only be her friend that day I saw you together in Jenner's.' Her own jealousy and hurt were over-riding common sense.

'No, that came later.'

'I see.'

'No, you don't. How could you?' He waited a moment before continuing. 'I went there that day to buy you a present and I ran into Jean quite by accident. She was very distressed, having just heard that her aunt was to have emergency surgery next day. I was trying to comfort her — that's all.'

While Jean, of course, was exploiting the situation, just as she did two days later when Staff and I went to visit poor old Agatha. . .'You could have explained,' said Tansy.

'I've already told you why I didn't.' He had unfastened his seatbelt and was leaning towards her.

'Not that it would have made any difference,' she insisted quickly. She had got the explanation of something that had been torturing her, only to reopen possibilities which could not be. 'Let's not rake over the past — it's all so pointless!'

'That being so, perhaps you'd like to tell me why you brought up the subject in the first place?'

In another second she would crack and that must not happen. There could be no future and the past was painful enough. 'Oh, stop it!' she cried, scrambling out of the car and plunging up the hillside, ripping her tights on the woody spikes of last year's heather roots as she went.

Struan caught up with her when she stumbled and fell over some twisted roots. He hauled her to her feet and didn't let her go. 'Oh, Tansy,' he breathed jerkily, as though it hurt just to say her name.

'It's no good. You don't understand. It's all quite hopeless.'

'Why?' he asked hoarsely.

He was unhappy and it was all her fault. 'There's something I should have told you right at the beginning, but I was too spineless — or too vain! I know your brother. We had an affair, but he left me to marry somebody else.' It was said at last. Tansy hung her head and waited for the storm.

'I'm so glad you found the courage to tell me,' Struan said quietly.

Her head came up sharply at that. She stared at him, unable to believe he had understood. 'Are you sure you heard what I said?'

'Quite sure.'

'Then why do you not rave at me — call me names? It's what I expected.'

'I was angry at first. Angrier than I ever was in my life before. I felt cheated, taken in. . . But I've done a lot of thinking since then.'

'You knew! When did you — find out?'

'Last week. While I was at home.'

'Oh, God — I'm so ashamed,' she moaned. 'I knew right at the start that I ought to tell you, or draw back. But I was in such a turmoil. Not that that excuses me. I cheated you — and I must pay for it.'

'If anybody cheated, I'd say it was Calum,' said Struan in the same quiet, controlled way.

'Are you saying that you don't blame me? But you must! How can you not? I was Calum's. . .' In her new honesty and self-abasement, she wanted to say 'whore', but the word wouldn't emerge. 'Mistress,' she croaked.

'You were Calum's dupe,' he corrected. 'Just as I was. Marie too — in a way.'

'Marie?' she whispered.

'The girl back home I'd thought of as mine — until Calum made her pregnant. She pretended she'd thought he was me. Can you believe that?'

'How long had she known you both?'

'Practically all her life.'

'Then no — it simply isn't possible.'

'Exactly.'

So Calum had betrayed them both, and Marie had betrayed Struan. She and Calum deserved each other. 'I don't know how you can bear to go near either of them,' she breathed.

'I can't in the normal way, but with a death in the family I couldn't avoid it.'

'What I don't understand,' she said slowly, 'is how my name came up.'

'Oh, that was Catriona. When my mother tried to find out, as she usually does, whether I was "seeing" anybody, as she puts it, Catriona told her about you. Unfortunately Marie was there too and, unaware of the connection, she later told Calum. He went completely berserk and called you every foul name under the sun. I didn't recognise the girl he was describing. When he grasped that you'd never mentioned him, he realised he'd given himself away for nothing. All he'd done was to show Marie what he really is.'

'No wonder you were so angry,' she whispered.

'Do you blame me?'

'Of course not—it's the most natural thing in the world. I'm just amazed that you can bear to speak to me.'

'I told you, I did a lot of thinking after that. And I tried to put myself in your place, tried to work out how you must have felt when confronted with the double of the man who had let you down. And gradually I came to understand why you acted as you did. You thought I was just another Calum.'

'Yes—I did,' she whispered.

His arms went round her and she didn't resist. 'And—now?'

'Now I know that you and Calum are as different as two men could possibly be.'

'But identical twins are said to be just that—identical in all respects.'

'Rubbish! You're living proof that's not true.'

'I hope you're as sure about that as you sound. I'd not like to think I was just—a substitute.'

'Oh, Struan—never! Never,' she repeated more quietly. 'Oh, I'll admit to being half afraid that was how

I saw you at first. Until I got to know you. Then I couldn't bear to think how much you would despise me when you found out what a fool I'd been. I thought we were — doomed. I think that's really why I made such a fuss about Jean. I was sure it had to end, and you had to have a reason, so — '

'Oh, my darling,' breathed Struan as his mouth found hers in a fever of longing and relief.

When he eventually let her go, Tansy was smiling.

'That's better,' he said. 'That's the way I like to see you.'

The smile became a laugh. 'We'd better not say anything about this in Ullapool, or Kirsty will think I'm trying to steal her thunder.'

'If Kirsty's half the girl I think she is, she'll know just by looking at us.'

'Oh, Struan!'

'Oh, Tansy!' But he was serious again now. 'You are — quite sure?'

'As sure as I'm hoping you are. . .'

'Then you couldn't possibly be more certain,' he breathed exultantly as they collapsed down into the heather. It wasn't all that comfortable, but they didn't notice that.

Mills & Boon

-MEDICAL ❤ ROMANCE-

The books for enjoyment this month are:

RED SEA REUNION Margaret Barker
HEART ON HOLD Lynne Collins
HEART CALL Lilian Darcy
A DOUBLE DOSE Drusilla Douglas

❤   ❤   ❤   ❤   ❤

Treats in store!

Watch next month for the following absorbing stories:

THE SPICE OF LIFE Caroline Anderson
A DANGEROUS DIAGNOSIS Jean Evan
HEARTS IN HIDING Alice Grey
LOVE IN A MIST Clare Lavenham